D0983497

THE
DREAMS
OF
MAIRHE MEHAN

JENNIFER ARMSTRONG

# THE

# DREAMS

# OF

# MAIRHE MEHAN

ALFRED A. KNOPF

NEW YORK

The excerpt from Walt Whitman's poetry on page 112–113
is taken from "Starting from  Paumanok" in *Leaves of Grass*, and the
song "*A Ghaoth Andeas!*" on page 69 is from *Songs of the Irish*
by Donal O'Sullivan.

THIS IS A BORZOI BOOK PUBLISHED BY ALFRED A. KNOPF, INC.

Copyright © 1996 by Jennifer Armstrong
All rights reserved under International and Pan-American Copyright Conventions.
Published in the United States of America by Alfred A. Knopf, Inc., New York, and
simultaneously in Canada by Random House of Canada Limited, Toronto.
Distributed by Random House, Inc., New York.

http://www.randomhouse.com/

*Library of Congress Cataloging-in-Publication Data*
Armstrong, Jennifer, 1961–
The dreams of Mairhe Mehan / by Jennifer Armstrong.
p. cm.
Summary: Mairhe, who lives in an Irish slum in Washington, D.C., in the 1860s,
struggles to come to grips with the impact of the Civil War on her family.
ISBN 0-679-88152-2
1. United States—History—Civil War, 1861–1865—Juvenile fiction.
[1. United States—History—Civil War, 1861–1865—Fiction.]
I. Title.    1996
[Fic]—dc20    96-4153

Printed in the United States of America
10 9 8 7 6 5 4 3 2 1

*First Edition*

*A note on the pronunciation of*
*Gaelic words and names in the text*

The most important word to pronounce is the name Mairhe, the Irish form of the name Mary. The vowel sound is pronounced approximately as "oi," thus, "Moira," although the actual sound of the name is hard to describe in words. *Dia dhuit* is pronounced "jia-gwitch," Badb is pronounced "Bove," and *slainte* is pronounced "slawncha." The name of the legendary hero Finn mac Cumhail is pronounced "Finn Macool."

# THE
# DREAMS
# OF
# MAIRHE MEHAN

# PROLOGUE

WERE THESE MY dreams? Were these then my brother's dreams?

Was I my dreams?

I'll tell you what happened to Mike in the night, of the three sounds of sorrow, of Lincoln's hornpipe, of my Da.

I was Mairhe Mehan, and these were my dreams. Or perhaps it may be they were my brother's.

Or perhaps they never were dreams at all. Their province is the edge of things, as it was mine: in the doorway, on the threshold, in the twilight, between one world and another.

So who can say if they happened or no? They're true enough, that I swear. They're woven tight and strong as any story is woven, thread following thread, the patterns emerging, the knots broken, the stitches dropped and reclaimed, the loose ends left or tied, the way we weave our own lives.

They are stories. I'll tell them.

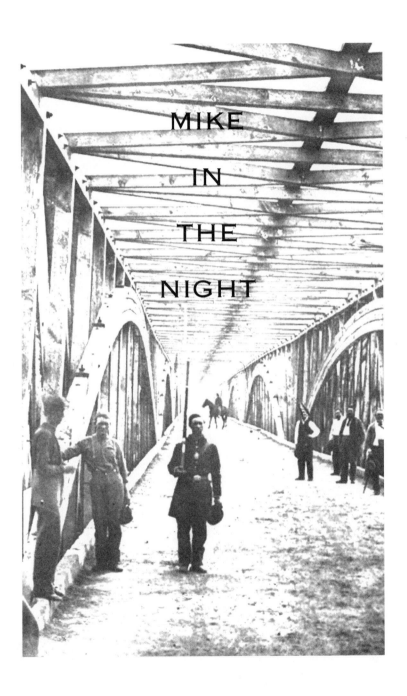

MIKE

IN

THE

NIGHT

# 1

TWO FEDERAL SOLDIERS stumbled out of a whorehouse on North Capitol Street, drunk as lords. One, a short sort with ginger whiskers, leaned over and began to puke in the gutter, and Mike, who was passing, began to laugh.

"Happy New Year to you," he said. He stamped through a puddle of muddy slush.

The one who could still stand stood still, and fixed Mike with an evil eye. "You damned Irish nigra. Get out of my way."

Mike bowed, and he knew the man would have at him, so he bulled forward, swinging his brickie bag to catch the soldier on the chin. All in a moment the man was on his back in the icy street.

Ginger stood up, stared at Mike, and then at his friend. "Boys!" he called over his shoulder.

The whorehouse door opened and a gust of infantry blew out with noise and whiskey fumes. Mike, ever a dancer, judged his card was too full and skipped away whistling, but the sounds of pursuit reached him and he began to run, down a dark alley, over a dung heap, vaulting a fence. A dog snarled out and slunk away and the wind sang in Mike's ears, and the light laugh rang out of him and ahead in the dark another noise began: glass breaking, a harlot shrieking, men laughing.

With unsteady breath and the grin of all devils, Mike pressed himself to the wall, and stole a view around the corner. Baker's boys, the Capital Police, were throwing bottles into the ashyard from the back door of another whorehouse. The smell of the liquor filled the cold air like the smoke of a battlefield, and a broad bawd screeched like a banshee and kicked men's shins.

Mike crept closer to the scene, well in the shadow, while the bottles burst like shells all around him. And when next the detective chucked a bottle over his shoulder, Mike sprang out and plucked it from the air and was gone again in the dark without breaking stride and the fellow looked back at the absence of smash.

Mike! Mike! The valorous fox, caparisoned horse, the dancer, the poet of deeds!

And so with a bottle he jigged his way back through Washington to Swampoodle, and there he found me, dreaming in my chair.

"Mairhe, girl, light us a fire, it's cold as the grave," he said, uncorking his bottle.

And I with my knees tucked up, and my black hair all down my back like a blanket, looked up at him with his glittering eyes. His throat moved as he swallowed.

"Don't let Da see what you've got," I told him.

I put aside the lace I was making, and stood and took his dinner from the shelf, and set it before him and stood and watched him eat. Mike attacked his meal like any wolf does. Between his bites and his parleys with the bottle, he told me of his day's work at the Capitol.

"And it was that cold the mortar hardly held, and the bricks like old kings' bones in your frozen hand, and the site boss was mad as a hornet for three men joined the Army last night and never came to work."

"Fools," I said.

Mike regarded me. "Fools how?"

"Fools to fight a war."

"Mairhe, girl, you're a girl."

"I know it, Michael Mehan. I've seen myself in the glass."

"And cannot have a political opinion in your head, so don't talk about things you don't know. The rebs—"

"The rebs?" came Da's voice.

He held himself upright in the doorway, and aimed one finger at Mike. "And why shouldn't the South break away? I ask you. Lincoln's no better than the English Crown, forcing itself and union onto Ireland."

Mike swung the bottle by the neck, his eyes on Da. "Ah, but now they say it's a war to free the slaves."

"Letting those blacks free will only drive down our wages," Da muttered, his eye following the bottle's arc.

"Whose wages?"

"I earn a wage!" Da roared. "I have been unable to work of late, is all!"

"Of late? I like that!" Mike shouted back, banging the bottle onto the table so hard that a gulp of whiskey pitched up through the neck and wet Mike's hand. "Late last summer, was it? You and your wild temper'd have us living in the street!"

"Don't *temper* me! Don't you *temper* me! No son of mine shall speak to me this way!"

"What'll you do, beat me? I'm not a child any longer, you're not stronger than me any longer!"

Da was white with rage. "In Ireland—"

"In *Ireland*? God help us!" Mike groaned. "What'd you bring us to America for, you crazy drunkard, if you love that country so much?"

And a thumping on the floor below us began, and a dog barked at the yelling and someone scolded in Gaelic. On the other side of the wall, someone coughed and cursed.

"Mike!" I stepped before him, and placed my hand over his eyes. I could feel them moving beneath my hand, could feel his angry breathing on my hand, and I whispered, "Go out."

He moved away from me, and headed for the door, but as Da took a step toward the bottle, Mike reached back and plucked it away. Da stood reaching for the empty air, and Mike was gone.

"Oh, my girl," Da said, easing slowly into a chair. His hands shook. "I've come a most unexpectedly long way down. Back in Sligo the Mehans were respectable, but then the Hunger came and who could stop it, then?"

"I know, Da." I straightened his coat, and he leaned back his head, his gray hair spilling over his collar like the strings of a broken harp. "I know."

"And where has your brother gone?"

I closed my eyes, and could see him in the street, clapping hands with his friends, linking arms with them as they began to march.

I dreamed my brother was gone for a soldier. When I cried out, Da shifted in his chair.

"What is it, then?" he asked.

I drew my coat about my shoulders. "Nothing, Da," I said. "Go to sleep."

"And where are you off to, girl, at this time of the night?"

I stopped at the door. "To work, Da. Remember? This is when I go to work."

"Oh. Yes," he said. "Yes." And subsided into himself with his chin on his chest and his dream was written plain on his face: Take me home. Take me back to my own country.

I slipped out the door. Down the dark stairs, feeling my way in the dark, I heard the wants of people living around us: more food, a better job, someone to love me, make my son good, take this cough from me. And try as I might, those were all plain to my ear, though I turned up the collar of my coat and stumbled in my haste.

Yet there at the doorway to the street did I pause, and look out at Swampoodle, where all those wants were multiplied a thousand thousand times. I didn't like to go out into them. But I went.

And what did I do but step in the mud the moment I gained the street? Mud, and frozen too, was everywhere in

Swampoodle. Why else such a dreary name? The Tiber Creek slouched through the neighborhood like a dirty drunk who won't leave, and sighed into our Swampoodle its damp, unlovely breath. Down the street I could see the lights from St. Aloysius making a halo around the church in the mist. An ambulance wagon was stuck in a muddy rut outside the door. The two drivers were swearing at the mules, which you might think were named Jesus and Mary from the way the men exhorted them.

I turned my back on the soldiers, and headed for the Shinny, cracking the ice in the ruts as I went in my muddy shoes.

The Shinny, now, what was it named for? For the broken shinbone of the old man, Dooley, who was host of the establishment? Or for the shindigs and shenanigans of the Irish boyos who leaned their elbows against the bar? Or for the pole on the roof many a man tried to shinny up to win a bottle of whiskey, and from which many a man had fallen? Who cared? said I whenever anyone asked. For to me the Shinny meant work, and that was all, and I didn't waste my dreams on it. I'd seen it at its best and worst, and there wasn't much difference between them.

Red-faced Mrs. Dooley was planted before the stove when I went in the back door. The frying pan before her hissed with sausage and peeled praties, and she poked at them with a fork. There was a roar of noise from the front of the house. New Year's Eve at the Shinny, and there must have been every able-bodied man in Swampoodle there.

"Mairhe, you're late."

"Sorry. Is my brother here?"

"Isn't he always?" Mrs. Dooley jabbed the sausages again. "Go on with you."

I put on an apron and went out into the saloon. Thick with smoke it was, and loud with the shouts of men and the crack of one man after the other pounding his glass down on the bar. Volleys of opinion shot back and forth through the fray, and a man howled out loud in the corner. A sign above the counter read, "No Soldiers Served." I ducked around behind the bar where Dooley was, and saw my brother Mike at home at the center of his fellows—O'Callahan, the O'Neill brothers, Milky Wesley with his bloody terrier, Snatcher, the scourge of Swampoodle's rats, nipping heels and ankles and sniffing among the sawdust of the floor.

"Start pulling," Dooley said for hello.

I grabbed a glass and held it below the tap, and pulled it full of ale.

Mike caught my eye and winked, and raised his glass to me. A pack of dog-eared cards was spread across the bar before him. I could see he was in the middle of a fine performance.

"It came to me today," he was saying. "Aren't there fifty-two cards to a deck? And fifty-two weeks to a year?"

A man beside him nodded the wise nod of a man in his cups. "To be sure. To be sure."

"And so it reasons, therefore, that each card must signify a week of the year." Mike held up the queen of hearts.

What a grin he had. "This lovely lady, now. She's the first week of summer."

"Go on with you, Mike." Another man stirred the cards with a dirty finger and plucked one out. "Here, what's the week for the two of clubs?"

"Second week of the year," Mike answered at once. "A lowly week, and a dark one, and a long way to go."

Dooley put his meaty elbows on the bar. "And the first week?"

"The first week?" Mike looked around. They loved him. He had drawn almost every man in the place. "Tomorrow begins the first week of January. It looks to the future, and has a bellyful of good plans and ambitions, but it's cold, boys. Very cold. Call it the ten of diamonds."

"More like the jack of spades, this year," called a man in the rear. "Taking Emancipation into the argument."

Someone else shushed him. "Be a good Christian, man. Where's your charity?"

Mike turned, eyes sparkling. "Jack of spades? That's what you say, Dick Finn?"

Fair-haired Finn moved forward into the fray. "I do. Them blacks'll take our jobs once they're free, every man jack of 'em, and it's a black day when that happens. Let 'em stay slaves is what I say."

"Get out, Finn, you drunken eejit! You can't see sense when it spits in your ear," cried Leary. "You've mistook the entire argument for this war!"

"I'm not drunk, Leary," Finn shot back. "I'm the soberest man here, I tell you."

"The black man is the Irishman's companion in the general disregard of the nation! They'll have *us* slaves next if we don't emancipate our African brothers!"

"Brothers my eye!"

Some shouted against Leary, and some shouted against Finn, and others shouted just to be making noise. Snatcher set to barking for the sport of it all. I sent Mike a look. He'd started it to make trouble, I did not doubt. It may be he hadn't guessed what trouble he'd start, but he knew he'd rouse a fight and he delighted in it. He turned away from the yelling and barking and leaned across the bar to me.

"How's about a glass while Dooley's popping his buttons?" Mike said, pushing his foam-ringed glass to me.

I pulled a glass for him. "Do you take a side in this argument?" I asked.

"Me take a side, Mairhe? Me?" He swallowed half his ale and belched discreetly into his hand. "I'm as fair and impartial as the day is long."

"Don't take a side," I warned my brother. "This war's none of our business."

"Now, my girl." Old Leary finger-pointed me straight. "It is indeed, for it is in our interest to test that a republic can survive such factioning and fractioning and come out whole. Else how can Ireland hope ever to make a republic of itself?"

"But the *Dublin News* is of the opinion that what was herebefore an unholy partnership is well disposed of." That was Mr. Lewes, who hooked his thumbs in his armpits and tucked in his chin. "And so leave it alone, let the South go, but don't fight for the slave states. Good riddance to them, let the republic restore itself without them."

"Here's the way of it," squint-eyed John O'Callahan was saying. He pounded on the bar to be heard. "This war's a training for us Fenians, and when we're practiced in the art of it, we're off to Ireland to rout the English. Those Irish sons who've no wish to go home and free the country are no Irish sons atall."

"Hear, hear!"

"And so it makes no difference to the Fenians which side you take, so long as you learn the trade of war?" Mike asked.

O'Callahan weaved a bit from side to side. He squinted harder at Mike. "What's that?"

"Which side do you take?" Mike asked.

"Whichever side'll have him!" Dooley said with a laugh. "And won't they be fighting to get such a specimen as our O'Callahan? Come, boys, it's New Year's Eve. Let's give politics a holiday."

The men broke up at that, and in the far corner two men with fiddles began scratching a tune. Milky caught up Snatcher in his arms and danced with him to the delight of the crowd, while the little ratter cocked his head one way and the other like a comical tiny man. Mike rested his cheek on his hand and smiled at me. He looked sleepy.

"Why do you do it, Mike?" I asked.

"What is it I do, sister darling?"

"Make trouble. Stir up fights. You're such an enemy to peacefulness and quiet."

"Fighting's my nature, sweet Mairhe. A man must fight."

I glared at him. "Don't come at me with that story. Only the foolish fight."

He smiled again, and rubbed his cheek against his hand like a tired hound. "You don't under—"

"I don't understand, I know, you've told me often enough," I broke in. "I understand you love to throw things into the air to see if they'll fall and smash, and I don't want you going off to try the war just to see the pieces break. It's none of our business. It's their fight, not ours."

"Why's that, Mairhe? Altogether Irish, are you? Pining for the dear old sod?"

"Not that."

"Ah, go home, little colleen. Go on with you. Take Da and go home. This is America. We want only the tryers and strivers here." He waved me away. "Off with the Fenians you go, back to the land of the forlorn and the faint hope."

There was a knot in me I thought might break, he pulled it so hard. "I'm not like Da. And I'm no Fenian. I've no plan to go back."

"Then you're American, is that right?"

I couldn't answer that. I had the excuse of needing to work, and I pulled glasses full of ale as rapidly as Dooley set them before me. Mike stayed where he was, for once out of the fray, and made circles on the bar with his finger.

The look of him made me want to weep, suddenly.

"Mike, what's the trouble?" I asked.

He made to smile, but instead he drew his breath on a sigh. "Mairhe, I'm tired."

"So're we all, Mike."

"Ah, but you sleep when you're tired. I don't sleep. I close my eyes, but it's nothing but darkness and fearful dreams tearing at my soul. I lift a plate of food, only to see it break into pieces in my hand. I try to build, but the bricks crumble as I lift them, stairs crack so I can't go up, I walk down a street looking for home, but the house turns to dust before my weeping eyes."

I touched his hand. "It's only dreams, Mike."

"I hate them. I hate the night, for that's when they come to me." The black hair fell across his eyes. He turned upon the crowded room, with the tramp of the men stamping with the music, the fiddlers poking the smoke with their bows, the devilish small dog snapping in circles and running at shadows. "And it's always the night with me," Mike said in a low, low voice. "And I'll never see a dawn."

# 2

IN THE NIGHT I dreamed I was a little girl with my Da, and we were going back to Ireland. We stood at the prow of a ship that leaped forward like any horse does, over the sea and its creaming waves, into the wind that smelled of grass. Da stood straight and tall, and he laughed down at me, his teeth white, his black hair streaming like a horse's mane.

"Look what I've got for you, my girl," he said, and drew from his pocket a doll of mine that had been broken, its leg snapped from its body by brother Mike. "It's whole again," he said.

"You've fixed it for me, Da?"

"And look. This and this," he went on, and pulled from all his pockets, and from the case that appeared at his side, all the broken things of my childhood: toys, and childish creations of wood and straw, and ripped clothes and tangled lace and a wounded bird that flew out from Da's hand and ahead of the ship, singing. "And this and this and this," Da kept saying as one after the other came new and whole.

And he laughed, and he was whole himself, and unbroken.

# 3

I WAS MAIRHE Mehan, and the truest thing I knew was I loved my brother, and that his heart was a good heart.

How could he have such a dream, then, when Emancipation came with the first day of 1863, and some Irishmen went hunting for a black man to hurt?

January 1: another cold day, and the brickies at the US Capitol were arguing with the Italian masons who did the lovely work of stone and sculpture on the new fine dome.

The brickies wished to work on the lee side of the building, and the masons wouldn't have them there, and the whole thing fell into argument and strife, for who wished to work on a day that should be a holiday? And down came the winter night so fast there was no more working anyway.

And off Mike went with the O'Neill boys, Jack and Dan, into the streets, where the caissons and the carts of artillery and the hospital wagons with their loads of broken soldiers had rutted the mud into frozen ridges. Pennsylvania Avenue was a mire, pitted and littered as a battleground.

"It's criminal," Jack said, his green eyes small with hate. "They've brought over those Italians and called them artisans. The fools don't even speak a language God can understand."

Mike had his head down against the wind, for he was tired, and the cold was aching him. The skin of his knuckles was broken and red, skinned where he'd fumbled the bricks in the clumsiness of cold. "Such a grand Capitol the government must have," he muttered. "A monument to the strength of my arm is what that building is."

"Nor are we welcome in it." Jack spit on the ground.

Dan made no comment. His was a dull mind, as all his fellows knew, and neither Mike nor his brother expected him to give an opinion. Dan strode through the wind, paying it no heed. His back was broad, and to Mike, who walked behind him, it looked like a stable door.

Government buildings at the side of the avenue echoed

the sounding of sentries' march. Cannons flanked this building and that, announcing the capital's fear of Lee. The general and his rebs were only over the river, skipping around Virginia like boys on a lark, while in winter camp at Falmouth the Union boys in the Army of the Potomac squatted in their shanties and cursed the mealworms out of their bread. New Year's Day and nobody was getting any joy of it, least of all Mike. Alongside Pennsylvania Avenue, the City Canal gave off a stink of garbage and dead cat.

The ground beneath their feet trembled and rumbled with the movement of distant wagons, giving its itch and its restless ache up into the Irishmen that walked the road. Mike felt it in himself, and saw it in the flex and stretch of Jack's hands, and in Dan's immovable back.

"Let's off to the President's House," Mike said with a wave, for up ahead all the distant length of the avenue was the shining white hideout of the leader of the Republic.

"I hate that Lincoln," said Jack.

"Jack hates ever'one," spoke Dan. And he laughed the sort of laugh a bull might make if it took it in its head to be mean.

"Lincoln's all right," Mike declared. "But he dresses like a bloody undertaker. Come on."

He hunched his shoulders against the cold. The wind blew cinders into his eyes as he pressed onward, and blew the black dust from a charcoal seller's wagon.

So Jack with his scowl and Dan with his milk-faced foolish frown followed after, plodding through the grit-blowing dark. And then they must share the avenue with the smart carriages and equipages pulled by polished horses with arched necks. The stream of traffic grew stronger and louder, and the current rolled on toward the President's House behind its oval of lawn trod bare by drilling soldiers and pastured beef. The house shot light through every window. The visiting throng pressed up the stairs as the leavers retreated. Inside, somewhere, a great gloomy man in black shook hands as he had done all day for the New Year's Reception, commander in chief of a noisy review to which all comers were welcome.

The Irish boys stood on the hard bare lawn where the carriages jostled for space, and blew into their hands. Mike danced from foot to foot, looking up at the white columns and the crowded steps and the pouring-out light, looking at the house where a poor farm boy was the President. "Go in, shall we? Let's do, they can't turn us out from a public reception. And it'd be fair warmer inside, I know that."

Dan stood where he was, planted like a stump. A driver shouted to him to move, but Dan never listened.

"Go on!" The driver yelled again. "Give way!"

The horses shied and shook their heads, unwilling to pass too close by Dan, looming statue that he was.

"Give way, man!"

"Oh, go shag yerself!" Jack shouted, all provoked.

"Damned Irish!" came the driver back. He cracked his buggy whip in the air. "Give way, you stupid Irish bull!"

Dan turned at last to look up at the man. Then he looked at Jack. Jack nodded.

Mike clapped his hands in Jack's face. "In! We're going in, Jack! Let's tell Lincoln what an old crow he is."

When nobody moved, the driver at last gave up in disgust and backed his roll-eyed horses. Jack was glaring up at the steps of the President's House. "I hate Lincoln," he said quietly. "I hate the Italians. I hate the Americans. And mostly I hate them."

And Mike looked where Jack was looking, and saw a black man coming down the steps, a tall hat on his head, pulling white gloves onto his hands. Laughing he was, and giving a good-night to a comrade at his side, and turning up the collar of his heavy cloth coat. Then he parted from his friend, and made his way past the military guards and the clusters of muffed and hatted ladies stepping into carriages, and so to the street. Jack took off after him, hands dug deep in his pockets. Dan followed dumbly behind his bad brother.

Mike stood where he was, in the shadow of a pillar, and then chased after his friends. None of them spoke, for the night was cold and their purpose was a stealthy one. Up ahead, the man in the tall hat walked with a joyous stride, swinging a cane, humming with gladness on this day of Emancipation, all unaware of the men following him in the dark. Voices fell away behind them. The street was empty but for them.

"Jack, let's find us a saloon," Mike said. He snapped a bare twig from a branch that overhung the sidewalk. "Let's us go to Foggy Bottom."

"Shut up."

The man ahead seemed to hesitate, and then walked on. Jack stopped, and Dan stopped, and Mike also. The man turned around. He stood straight.

"Who is it?"

Nor Mike, nor Jack, nor Dan spoke. They were all in the night.

"I am Dr. Mason," the man said. "Do you have business with me?"

Jack stepped forward where a light fell onto him. "You and your kind," he made in answer.

"Come away," Mike said.

Jack heeded him not at all, and Dan stepped forward with his brother. Mike saw the doctor's shoulders sag with the heaviness of it all.

"I am not carrying money," the doctor said. "Do not accost me. There's nothing to gain."

Jack and Dan went forward with no more words. Mike saw the lie of the land and liked it not at all, and he turned and slipped back into the shadows and was gone. He ran into the dark, cutting north toward Swampoodle, and the night chasing him all the way.

# 4

DA WAS IN fine fettle an evening or so after the New Year. He rose from an afternoon's sleep with a mind for mending.

"I've a good feeling about tomorrow," he said as he sat

at the table across from me. "Give us some tea, daughter."

"Kettle's just on. It'll be a minute." I was working at some lace before heading for the Shinny. Ten cents a yard it fetched, but hard on the fingers were those ten cents.

Da sat and watched me, and the kettle ticked and muttered on the stove behind me. Da drummed his fingers on the table. I looked from below my lashes, at his drumming fingers. So scarred and bent they were, so worn and the nails so cracked and yellow.

"I believe tomorrow is a day I'll find work."

I stopped in my work, then went on, my fingers never halting. I chose not to look at him. "Ah, is that right, Da?"

"Yes. I do believe so. A man should bestir himself at the start of a new year. All things are possible to a man who only strives."

"That's sure."

"And I know, my girl, that you've had a worry for me. But those jobs I had were the wrong jobs, and the bosses against me, every man of them. I'll find a job I can stick with. Something worthy of a Mehan. Worthy."

"I know it, Da."

"That's right. I'll show them. I'll show them all what an Irishman can do."

I ducked my head lower over my work. "Yes, Da."

"Ah, Mairhe. Did I ever tell you of what happened to me at Sligo Fair, when as a young man, I was considered the finest fighter in Connacht?"

The kettle fussed, and the distant shouts of an argument and laughter downstairs were like the shouts of farmers at market fair, of sheep and kine crying on the road to auction. I knew this story. Of Matthew Mehan, handsome fellow, kicking the straw from his way and stooping under the ropes to meet the challenger, while the assembled folk laughed and clapped and laid their wagers, and a cool breeze off the ocean tossed the fine dark hair into Matthew's eyes. And behind all heads a sky so blue, and the clambering hills so mossed with green.

Da scraped his chair back, and stretched out his hands to clasp behind his neck. For a few moments we were quiet. I wished I might only work on my lace; my fingers knew the knots to make, my bobbin knew what holes to dance through. The slender threads clung to one another and grew slowly forward like lichen across a gray stone.

Da cleared his throat. His faded eyes sought mine with a plea.

"Yes, tell me about it, Da," I said at last.

He sighed, happy, and leaned back for storytelling. "It starts long ago in the time of Turloch O'Connor, and him so brave. Such a wild spalpeen of a lad, but the King of Connacht nonetheless, and took the O'Connors into war against the English at the Battle of Athenry."

"Yes, Da."

"And so with clash of halberd and pike, and the archers making a rain of arrows, and the ground thick with heart's blood. And in the midst of it all, one Brian Mehan of the Mehans saw his eldest son gored fornent his very eyes, in the hesitation of his heart. And from that day, Mehan swore to raise up his sons to be fighters who never hesitate, and never lose.

"In 1316 that was, but even so it was that as a lad, I too was raised to fight. And I used my fists against all comers in the ring. Every fair and market that cared to put up a purse saw me there, ready to fight. Never did I fail to win a bout, my girl. Never."

"No, Da," I murmured, my eyes on my lace. "No, sure you didn't."

"And it was there at Sligo Fair that I first saw your mother, laughing and colloguing with her friends over a table of brass candlesticks. *Mavrone!* What a darling she was."

The kettle was chattering on the stove. I turned away from Da to stop him from speaking. Who can hear the same dream over and over without her heart breaking? I poured water into our jug pot, onto the old tea leaves that still sulked there, and let the steam bathe my cheeks.

Da was shaking his head and smiling. "No, no. A Mehan never loses. Fighters always. We pick our fights, and we never turn aside. True Irishmen. True to Ireland."

A silence came between us, and I dared not look into his eyes. Where was Mike? we neither of us asked. What fight was he fighting now? Where was he in the darkness of this night?

I sat down again with my lace, and measured my progress against my arm. Five cents. A few handspans of white web. Not much to cling to, was it?

And then in came Mike, and pulled out a chair while

we sat without words to watch him, and he crossed his arms before him.

"I've signed papers and joined the Federals," said he. "I'll be leaving in a month for Falmouth."

"Jesus, no," said Da. "You're an Irishman."

And the bobbin fell from my fingers, and the stitches in the lace came all undone, raveling out from my senseless hands.

# 5

I DREAMED I was at the Capitol, where the 8th Massachusetts was quartered in the Rotunda. It was dark inside, and the lamps smoked to make my eyes sting. I went from officer to officer, soldier to soldier, asking who'd done this terrible thing to my life. One officer, seated at a table, held a map to the lamp's light. He tipped the map this way and that to the light and frowned, as though there were some will-o'-the-wisp feature engraved there that only showed from one angle, and that he could not see for more than a moment.

"Was it you?" I asked.

This officer in his blue and braid did not look up. He did not hear me. Above his head, the Rotunda dome echoed with coughs, and the stamp of boots, and the rattle of rifles stacked together. Someone was brushing boots with a *sh-sh, sh-sh*. The officer turned down the lamp and rose from the table. I followed, and we passed out through a doorway into a dim corridor, where senators leaned against the wall in weariness, showing one another their bills and urging support.

"My brother's job is working here. He's helping to build this Capitol for the government," I told the officer, tugging on his sleeve. "He's not to go to war. He's to stay here and build."

The officer walked on, his saber banging against his leg. And then, at the far end of the corridor where a door led into darkness, he turned, and he was Mike.

"You'll never change my mind," said he. "I won't ever be moved in this."

He smiled. And then he went through the doorway into the night, leaving me there alone on the other side.

# MEETING

# MR.

# WHITMAN

# 1

THE NOONTIME SHINNY was loud in my ears. I was attempting to clear a basin of dirty plates from the tables when Mr. O'Callahan came in, waving a two-cent newspaper like a flag. I went on with my work as he began.

"Listen to this, now, lads!" O'Callahan called. "Queen Victoria has addressed the Parliament on the question of 'the hostilities in the North American States.' "

"What's she say then, the old cow?"

There was a roar of laughter at Lewes's remark.

O'Callahan straightened his paper with a snap and read in a high, quavering voice. " 'We have abstained from attempting to induce a cessation of the conflict between the contending parties,' says she. 'Because it has not yet seemed to Her Majesty— ' er, I should say 'My Majesty,' " O'Callahan corrected himself. He winked at me.

"Go on, John," Dooley called from the bar.

"To continue," O'Callahan said. " 'It has not yet seemed to Her Majesty that any such overtures could be attended with a probability of success.' "

I hitched the full basin up onto my hip. "That's wisdom."

"Oho!" O'Callahan looked around at his friends, eyes wide, and then returned to me. "How's that now, Miss

Mairhe Mehan? How do you come by such an under-
standing and sympathy with Queen Factoria?"

"Nothing will stop men from fighting one another if
they've made up their minds to it," I said. "What's the
good of reasoned arguments? I'm having no part of it,
myself. Excuse me." And so I pushed by the men and into
the kitchen.

And there, Mrs. Dooley stood as ever at her hissing
stove.

"Give over, missus," said I. "I'll take a turn pushing the
praties around if you like."

"Oh, Mairhe, good girl." Mrs. Dooley sat heavily down
in her chair by the door, and fanned her hot face with her
apron. "Those sausages are for Mr. Finn, now. He likes 'em
cooked dry through and through."

And so down I set the dishes with a thump, and took up
the fork. In truth I liked it better in the kitchen, where the
voices didn't shout so. I frowned down in the pan, poking
the sausages and the praties, and glad to be out of the
yelling in front.

"And how's your Da?" Mrs. Dooley asked, catching her
breath in a gulp. "He doesn't come around anymore."

"No, missus, he's not feeling much his usual self and
likes to bide at home."

"Ah, for shame. We've forgiven him these many
months for breaking our door when he lost his last job,
Mairhe, tell him that. He needn't be shy to come back."

"He's only feeling low," I said, the shame of it in my
own face.

Mrs. Dooley stretched her legs before her and sighed. "Such a pity. He was ever a handsome man, Matthew Mehan. I call to mind the night he first came in here, so big, with that fine silver hair wild about his head and a fine beard and his blue eyes all smiling."

I nodded, for that was the father I dreamed in my dreams. A strider and a striver, and free with gesture and laughter both.

And then the door opened, and such a man walked in with a buffet of noise from the front of the house. Tall, and broad about the shoulders and shod in polished boots. This was the man my father was once.

"Mrs. Dooley?"

Mrs. Dooley and I only stared at the man conjured by our conversation. Before me on the stove a sausage popped and hissed. The man closed the door and looked at us.

"Mrs. Dooley?" he asked again.

"Yes, oh, to be sure," the woman replied, struggling to rise and fussing her apron. "What is it you're wanting, mister?"

He waved toward the door behind him. "Mr. Dooley says you know one Mrs. Pyle?"

"Kitty Pyle?"

"Kitty Pyle, yes. I have a charge to bring her the effects of her soldier grandson, who just last night died in the hospital. He said he had kin here in Washington City, and begged me bring his poor things to her."

Mrs. Dooley was all on guard in a moment. She eyed the man up and down. He wore no uniform nor insign.

"You're an army doctor, then?"

"No, I only sit with the boys, and read to them and do their small errands and write their letters. See, I've written what address he knew—" And the man took from his pocket a sheaf of paper folded together and stitched with rough string on one side to make a book no larger than his hand. His broad thumb flipped the pages. "Mrs. Kitty Pyle, Swampoodle. It's all he knew. I can't make my way in this neighborhood."

Mrs. Dooley worked her lips in grave thought. She turned my way. "You take him, Mairhe. Mrs. Pyle lives round by Haney's."

The big man with the wild white hair looked from her to me and back again, his eyes wide and waiting.

I took my coat from its nail. "Follow me, mister." And went out the back door into the alley.

"Moira, is it? Myra?"

"Mairhe, yes," I replied, skirting empty crates, leading the way. Above the alley, a strip of high blue sky showed cold.

"I've only been in Washington since December. My brother was wounded at Fredericksburg and I came down to nurse him. Can't say I know my way around the whole city, yet. I've walked a good bit of it, but not Swampoodle."

"No reason to."

"I don't know," he said, stopping to gaze down a side street. "Any place with as fine a name as Swampoodle must have plenty to recommend it."

"I wouldn't recommend it, myself."

Our way led up the miry street to Cabbage Alley. Somewhere in the distance was a crack of gunfire from soldiers drilling, and the street was crowded with wagon traffic, and oxen complaining. I trod through the mud with the white-haired man lingering and looking along behind me.

He walked quiet and quick for a big man, and considered all around him with a curious eye. I watched him looking at the crowded window of a pawn shop, where sat a dainty harp in a copper cook pot. He smiled happily, and caught my eye.

"Music makes an excellent meal. I've dined on it many times and never felt hungry."

"I wonder how you came to be so big, then," I replied.

He put his head back and laughed. "I always eat a big breakfast. Lead on, Miss Mairhe."

And so we went along, skirting the worst of the puddles and the horse dung, and came abreast of St. Aloysius. Orderlies were unloading a wagonload of bread, lifting the baskets high and picking their way across the mud. My charge paused and looked up at the bold clock tower.

"Your church?" he asked.

"It's a hospital, now," I replied. "I don't go in anymore."

We walked on past it. I did not look. Ambulance wagons waited around the corner at another door. I kept my eyes down, and kept a sharp watch for puddles. From the church-turned-hospital came the smell of chloroform, and blood, and men weeping.

"Why not?"

I glanced his way. His breath fogged from his lips.

"Why not what?" I asked him.

He halted, and waved back at St. Aloysius. "Why don't you go in? It's still a house of worship, if you choose to worship in a house."

"It's a house of fighters in pain. I won't worship there."

I clutched my coat tight around me. The cold was stealing up through the soles of my boots. My cheeks stung. The man didn't move.

"Sir. Mrs. Pyle is this way."

He still didn't move, but looked at me from below his brushy brows. "To my way of thinking, it's much holier now for the pain those fighters feel."

The stillness between us was broken by a scream from inside the church. I turned away and stumbled to be going, catching myself against the wall of a building as I went. "Not to my way of thinking. If you'll just follow me, sir."

"My name is Walt, Mairhe."

"This way, Mr. Walt."

He trudged along through the mud beside me. "They're good boys, all of them."

"Who's that, Mr. Walt?"

"The soldiers. You should go in sometime and visit with them. They're so lonely, you could do such good just to say hello."

I stopped by Haney's smithy.

"Sir, I will not go into the hospital. You've no call to scold and upbraid me this way."

He raised his eyebrows. "That's a strong reaction."

I looked away. "Mrs. Pyle is just in that house, through there," I said, pointing at the end of an alley.

Mr. Walt was a big reproachful bear beside me, chin sunk on his chest, and arms folded. His cheeks were red with the frost, and the rims of his ears. I wanted to push him down the alley. I wanted him to go away.

"Thank you for bringing me here, Mairhe. Mrs. Pyle's grandson was a good boy. He was brave before he died. He wanted his sister."

I breathed hard. "I am sorry for it."

He moved down the alley. In the distance, there was another round of gunfire.

I ran back to the Shinny by the long way around, so I wouldn't see the hospital again, and when I burst in through the kitchen door, Mrs. Dooley gave me the wide eye.

"What's gotten into you? You look that scared, I swear you're white as a pratie."

Carefully, carefully, I shut the door behind me, shut out the sounds of the war that were out there, everywhere. I wouldn't take a part in it, not for anything would I aid and succor the men who were breaking each other to bits. Mike wanted to break the best thing of all, now, and that was himself, and I hated him for it.

"Didn't try an impertinence with you, did he? That man?"

"No, missus." I blew on my hands to warm them, and rubbed them together over the stove.

Mrs. Dooley lifted a burner and jabbed her poker down in the fire, and the flames leaped up with a shower of sparks. In a moment was a dream before my eyes of men sitting around a fire, hunched in their oilcloth capes, their blue caps pushed low on their brows and a pot of coffee hissing and spitting into the embers.

"I'd like to find my brother, if you won't need me for a bit."

"Go on. Mind you don't stay away too long."

And so I left the Shinny again.

That was the first time that I met Mr. Whitman. I was soon to meet him again, though it was long before I'd know who and what he was to me. Seldom do we see through the shadows in our dreams when first we awake in the morning.

## 2

MIKE WAS AT the Capitol. The day was sore and bitter, and the brickies were compelled to do heavy labor, as the mortar wouldn't hold. He and the O'Neill boys were working in the shadow of the new dome, which rose like a skeleton above them.

Tall was the building, and stretching its wings out on either side to gather us all in its big embrace. The dome was like the sketch of an eagle's egg, waiting to be hatched, and the scaffolding holding it up like the twigs and sticks of a giant nest. Laborers were everywhere, nursing the thing to term. I could hold my hand before my face and block entirely the shape of that dome, yet between my fingers was a glimpse and another glimpse—it was a sight not to be blocked.

And oh, what an urgent and impatient Republic it was, that filled its Capitol to overflowing before the building was even complete. Senators and lawyerly men and soldiers and masons milled about the place like ants of an anthill, and the great congressional house built itself piece by piece into the blue air, as though the men who swarmed about it were transforming themselves into bricks and iron and stone to give the place shape.

On the grounds, a regiment was drilling, marching in file as a sergeant barked and brayed. I saw Dan punch Mike in the shoulder and laugh. Then did Mike catch sight of me, and ran to join me where I stood at the edge of things, my hand still lifted to the building.

"*Dia dhuit*," he said, and made me a bow. Jesus be with you.

"Don't mock me with your Irish hellos," I said.

"They say there's a rare little man at the President's House."

I laughed at his suddenness and quicksilver changing, and took his hands in mine to chafe them warm. "I always heard he was a great tall man."

"No, girl, today General Tom Thumb is to visit the President. Let's see if we can't spy him out." He danced me around.

"Mike, what are you about? Haven't you a job to do?"

He winked over at the shadows of the dome where Jack and Dan toiled. "The foreman can shag himself. I'll be joining my regiment in two weeks, so the job can go to blazes."

I had to laugh, but wouldn't let him drag me along yet. "But you might change your mind and give up that idea, and so you'll need to keep your job."

"No. No. A thousand thousand times no, Mairhe, enough with your coaxings and claimings. Come along with you now. And for the matter of that," he added, cocking his head and fixing me with his grin, "what of your own job?"

"The Shinny can bide without me for a bit. How many times does an Irish girl get to see a tiny, tiny man? For all our own men are such giants and heroes in our eyes."

"Saucy harlot you are."

And so we went smiling up the avenue, all the while Mike telling me what he'd heard about the little man from Mr. Phineas T. Barnum's cavalcade of wonders, and how the little general had married his little lady love, and they were the tiniest pair and could go sailing in a teacup and paddle themselves about with silver spoons, and how Willard's Hotel was drawing the crowds to see the two wee grandees take their coffee of a morning.

"But we'll catch sight of them going in to see the old black crow," Mike said, and giving a wide smile to a matron as we passed.

"You've got a liking to look at the President's House," I said to him.

"Perhaps I do."

"Perhaps you think you'll live in it yourself one day."

"Ha, that an Irishman should do that," Mike laughed. "We're good for soldiers, not commanders."

I frowned. "Never say so."

A sparrow flicked into the street and away, and I followed it with my eyes to see a column of marching soldiers. My stomach turned. I'd suddenly the wildest wish to see General Tom Thumb and his miniature bride, all cheer and marvel. I'd a wild wish to get away from the sight of soldiers.

And so we joined a crowd standing outside the white mansion, and there was laughing and jokes, and a fat man with a voice from Boston read from a newspaper about the wedding ceremony (Mr. Barnum presiding), and there were many guesses how far up Lincoln's longshanks leg the general would stand, or what number of chairs and tables he'd have to climb to look Lincoln in the eye. And didn't Mike have to join in with the guessing and joking, and didn't he soon have all of a crowd around himself watching him and listening to him, rogue that he was.

And the fat man's fat wife, bundled in a black bonnet, screeched with jolly laughter and patted her cheek. "Don't say so!" she begged with tears standing on her lashes. "Don't say so!" Beside her, a man with a wide Ohio accent and sandy side whiskers offered his lunch around—a dented pail of tawny biscuits—and three solemn girls as alike as three new potatoes in their russet hats and capes said in chorus, "Where's General Thumb, for we've hemmed tiny

41

hankies for him!" The weather was fine and fair and frosty, and the spirit of holiday warmed the crowd in their boots and their scarves. I saw two lovers kiss, and a woman cradle her pink babe at her shoulder. And so Mike went on, composing a very ballad of General Thumb as he stood there, and I, laughing with the rest of them, stepped back to the edge of the crowd and saw again the same white-haired man so like my father walking past, and he saw me.

"Well, Mairhe, I didn't imagine to meet you again today or ever." Mr. Walt hailed me from the middle of the street and strode near. The living breath puffed from him like steam from a train as he came.

"My brother." I gestured toward Mike. "We came to see the midgets."

Mr. Walt's eyes widened. "Is that right? All these people are here to see General Thumb?"

He turned to regard the noisy crowd. The faces, all the faces, were bright with cold and with laughing. The Ohio man. The fat Boston man and his fat wife. The pink babe and the hanky girls. And my brother, at home amongst them all like their own darling son or brother. Mr. Walt smiled, and smoothed down his beard. "Beautiful, aren't they?"

"Sir?"

"All the population in their coats and mittens, joining on the street outside the President's House, meeting their fellows together. Talking and talking, like one body with many voices." Mr. Walt spread his arms wide. "The farmer, the mechanic, the fisherman, the country doctor and the city doctor, the young mother and the old mother, east west, north south . . . I like to come here, myself, and look at him," he added suddenly, rounding on me.

I was surprised. "Look at who? Tom Thumb?"

"Lincoln. I have rooms over on K Street nearby Lafayette Square, and so I like to think us neighbors."

"You might call on him at teatime, then," I suggested.

He smiled at me. "I might. He's a common man. But one of the uncommonest kind. Too busy for a clerk like me to pester him, though."

Mr. Walt beamed at me, and listened to the crowd, and I couldn't recall why he'd frightened me so. He was a goodly man.

"Mr. Walt—"

Smiling still, he nodded as though in answer to a question. Then he held out his hand and I shook it.

"I'm off to Armory Square hospital, on my regular rounds as a roving beside-the-bed sitter," he said to me. "There's a Brooklyn boy had his leg shot off. I know his family. I promised to take him an orange."

And he dug in his pocket and brought out an orange from the Carib, gleaming and bright and round in his calloused hand. He tossed it up, and I followed it into the air with my gaze until it disappeared into the glary dazzle above us.

I blinked, and shielded my eyes. But Mr. Walt kept his hand out, and in a moment it fell into his palm again. Then there he went through the yawping, yammering, gift-giving American crowd, a big dreamy man with a sun in his hand.

### 3

ONCE UPON A time were twin brothers, dearer to their father than cream from a lovely cow, dearer than dew on a pasture, dearer than the curve of a baby's cheek. The father was king of a fair and wide domain, and much taken up with the wise management of it. Yet upon his death the succession had not been arranged, and so the two boys set-tled on ruling together.

But one had ideas for the sovereignty of this land that did not concur with the ideas of the other brother. Soon discussion led to argument, and a division of lands where one would hold sway over the other. It wasn't of course a plan that could work, and before much time had passed from the father's death, the country went to war on itself.

And what was the natural outcome of war but the death and destruction of all that the two brothers loved? Each brother in his camp asked his own oracles to name the one blow that would cripple the other army. And each oracle said: Kill your brother, murder his family, salt his wells.

So heartsore were they two that upon that instant they laid down their weapons, and sought one another and embraced one another, swearing never to make war again.

This was the way that peace came back to that domain: learning that the only route to victory was to crush his brother foe utterly was a road none wished to travel.

◎━◄·   ◎━◄·   ◎━◄·

This, of course, is not a story about the United States of America.

Nor is it a story of Ireland.

# 4

I WAS IN the Shinny of a dark afternoon later in the month, working my lace and listening to Dooley tell us a battle tale of Finn mac Cumhail, and from down the bar came interjecting the reports of how Mr. and Mrs. Lincoln were marking the one-year anniversary of their son Willie's death, as read from the paper by Ditty O'Herlihy, and I wove it all together into my lace.

" ' . . . is said to be spending the day in prayer . . . ' "

" . . . and the stones of the road calling out that here lay his son beneath them . . . "

" ' . . . while the Secretary of War read dispatches in the next room . . . ' "

" . . . and the ax broke into pieces in the father's hand, and he tore the silver hair from his head at the death of his son . . . "

" ' . . . but a parent's grief must give way to the urgency of the hour . . . ' "

" . . . and the warrior king broke his shield in four and threw the pieces to the points of the four winds . . . "

" ' . . . and subordinate personal loss for the good of the country in this time of war and national loss . . . ' "

" . . . before losing his heart entirely and wandering

the land all the rest of his days, calling on the name of his son . . . "

And just as this country and all our legends and heroes were falling to pieces, so was my own family. For in rushed our neighbor Maud Shea, pale as a banshee, screaming to me as she clutched the air.

"Mairhe! Your father! Such a fit this time! He's wrecking the place!"

"Jesus and Mary." I was out the door and running, and the population of the Shinny running behind me too, like the ragged hem of an old woman's dress, dragging along in the mud.

The light was fading into a weary winter twilight, and the dimming sky above the street was an easier road to follow than the dark path at my feet. The blood of my heart beat a stumble against my ears. Yet it wasn't loud enough to cover the sound of breaking and crashing that drew me around the corner to find a crowd outside our building, and see the crockery, clothes, and chairs come flying through the window above. At each missile the crowd would draw away, and then press in again to pick up and pick over the broken shards of my family's household. Above it all, blurry and far away, was the yelling of my Da.

I took the stairs with my throat tearing on each breath. Another crowd filled the stairwell and clustered on the landings: women stretching their shawls around bony shoulders, grimy children with round black eyes. The yelling came clearer as I dragged myself up.

"Take it! Take it for we'll not need it anymore!"

How could such a poor household as ours have enough to throw from a window for more than two minutes together? Yet there was Da when I went into the room, dragging the drawers from the dresser, and tipping them out into the street. My own silver-headed Da was throwing our lives to the four winds.

"My father!" cried I. "My father, no!"

He stumbled and turned around, and his face broke into a glad smile. The whites of his eyes were shot red. "Mairhe, daughter! I can use your help." And he went for the dresser again but I stood myself before it.

"What are you doing!"

"We're leaving, Mairhe," he said, catching his breath and looking pleased. "Gave up the rooms. And I'll never regret leaving this dirty hole, either," he added with a broad kingly gesture of disgust.

My ears were ringing. "My father, why did you give up the rooms? Where is it we'll live?"

"No, no, Mairhe. No no." And he was shaking his head, and trying to get past me to pull out a drawer. "We're selling all this and going home to Connacht."

I stood my ground, and he squinted and tried to get by me but couldn't, and I thought I might cry, or vomit on the floor. The place looked like a land where a war's been, all things upended and disarrayed, every pitiful thing we owned burst from its rightful place and ruined. Mugs, plates, bowls lay in shards, clothes and cloths hung or lay about like the lifeless hulls of slain soldiers, coal was strewn about the floor like shrapnel.

Da gave up trying to get by me, and stood regarding his work with a critical eye. He nodded, and bent to pick up the leg of a broken chair. He walked with a ruined grace, a crippled boxer with no one to fight but himself.

"My father, we're not going home."

"We are."

Where the window was, the light was giving up and going away. In the corners of the room where the dark was, the edges of my life were blurring. Da stood where he was, hefting the broken chair leg in one hand, testing its weight like a war ax.

There was a noise behind me at the door. Dooley was there, and John O'Callahan, old friends both of my Da. Someone behind them held a lamp, and its light seeped in around their heads like something leaking from an old glass.

"Matthew."

Dooley came toward Da, kicking the broken things out of his way. I feared Da would strike at him with the stick, but Da only looked at his friend. Dooley took him by the arm, and led him out into the hall. O'Callahan stepped aside as they came, and walked in to me, nervously rolling his eyes this way and that at the spectacle of battle fought within the walls.

"Mairhe, they say he did give up the rooms, and they're already let," O'Callahan whispered. "Can't stay on here."

"Where's Dooley taking him?"

"To St. Aloysius, see if they'll take your father in on the

parish," O'Callahan continued in the same awed whisper. He looked about in the dimness and whistled. "Sh'll I get my wife to help you take up your t'ings, Mairhe?"

I hung my head. I saw nothing to save. "No, thank you, Mr. O'Callahan. There's nothing here, now."

So I left the rooms and went feeling my way down the stairs like any old woman does who's seen the power of destruction let loose in her life. Dooley and my Da were just leaving the house through the curious crowds. I stopped in the doorway to watch them, and then followed them out and down the street toward St. Aloysius.

As we neared the church, its strong lights threw a gleam around my Da's white head, and around Dooley like a brawny ambulance man propping him up. And forward they two went to the side door of the church. I saw the door open, and the robed figure of the chaplain, and Dooley's head moving as he spoke.

And then was my Da welcomed in, and he went in with the rest of the wounded and crippled soldiers and the door closed behind him. I could not move from where I was, though Dooley looked back at me and then came my way.

"Come on, girl, you'll stay at the Shinny. Mrs. Dooley loves you like a daughter anyway. You'll come see your Da tomorrow."

That I doubted, though I didn't speak my doubt to Dooley.

# 4

AND WHERE WAS Mike for all of this? Croosheening in the ear of a pretty girl he met outside Willard's Hotel, when he was hanging about to see the officers and learn a military swagger. He was to go to Falmouth in the morning, and damned if he wouldn't spend his last night as a free man spinning some kind of yarn for a pair of fair blue eyes.

"Say you'll walk with me along the river," he begged. "Yours may be the last sweet face I take to war with me."

This Ellie Anderson showed him her dimples. "Are you really joining your regiment tomorrow?"

"I am." Mike showed the way toward the Potomac, and they fell into step. He knew when to speak, and when not to. He gazed ahead, into the winter sunset, a look of tragedy on his face.

"I think you're awful brave," Ellie said. "Aren't you scared of going into the war?"

Mike shrugged a no. "I come from a long line of soldiers, Ellie. My father and grandfather and so back and back fought beside all the great American patriots. We're one of the oldest soldiering families in the land. A Mehan doesn't know fear."

"But I thought you were an Irish boy!"

"Did you?" Mike guided her around a puddle and they stood by the Chain Bridge.

Her eyes were downcast. She feared she had insulted him. "Your accent. You sound like an Irish boy."

"The accent lingers in the family," Mike told her with a laugh. "And I've lately spent time among the poor of Swampoodle, learning their ways and gaining the trust of those I will lead. I suppose it brings out the Irish in my voice."

They stood at the bank of the black river by the heavily guarded bridge. A cold wind pressed against them. Ellie shivered, and drew her coat closer, and drew nearer Mike, who made his own warmth.

"Your family must be proud," she said.

"I only do my duty." Mike waved one hand to take in the river and the opposite shore. "Our country. Father never ceases to speak of it. It is his most ardent wish that I defend it."

Ellie looked at him. The setting sun put gold on his cheeks. No doubt she thought he was a marvel.

"And your mother? Doesn't she mind awfully?"

"She died— no," he added when Ellie cried out. "It was long ago, in a smallpox epidemic. She left our fine house and went among the people of Swampoodle who were suffering so, and she nursed and cared for them, never giving a thought to her own health and strength."

"Ah." A sigh passed Ellie's red lips. "Your whole family then is a family of brave heroes. And so much on behalf of the poor Irish."

Mike stooped to pick up a rock, and he chucked it at a stick that went floating past. "They're much despised, the poor Irish. I see them sometimes at work on the Capitol, where they lay bricks. How valiant they are to me, laying the foundation for our nation's greatest building. A great testament and symbol of union is what it is, and they construct it proudly."

"And now you're going to war to preserve the Union," Ellie whispered. "Oh, Mr. Mehan—"

"Mike, call me Mike—"

"I think you're wonderful, Mike."

Mike chucked another rock, and allowed himself a modest smile. "A man must fight for something, or he must fight against himself."

"And does your father have a command, now?"

"Does he?" Mike laughed. "Try to keep him at home! He's ferocious in battle."

He put an arm about her shoulders, and pointed her ahead with a wave of his hand. "Picture him, Ellie," (and so she did) "a tall, broad-shouldered man with the mane of a lion, white as moonlight, a warrior-poet striking at his enemy, laying waste all around. Fearless, he feels no pain, the cries of his foes touch him not, he is the whirlwind."

He stopped speaking and let the air cool his cheeks. Up the river came a barge, its deck covered with the shadowy forms of silent soldiers from the Union Army's camp at Falmouth. Ellie pressed one hand over her heart.

"I feel a great honor in listening to you speak," she said in a low voice. "It makes me feel proud to be American, to hear how you talk. Your father must be so proud to know what you'll do to protect this country."

Mike grinned. "You should see the effect it has on him.

Nothing matters to him more than the land of his birth. Why, when I left home today, he could barely speak, so moved was he."

And Mike started to laugh, while the barge of silent soldiers went silently by.

# THE
# IRISH
# BRIGADE

# 1

A THOUSAND AND half a thousand more years ago, the Fianna were the soldiers of Ireland, with Finn mac Cumhail at their head. And the ages wore on, and the rough stones of Ireland were worn smooth by the tears of the Fianna's families. Badb, the great gory goddess of war, washed soldiers' clothes in the moss-rocked streams by the fields of battle, and each man who saw her wash his garments knew his blood was forfeit, and threw himself ever more fiercely into the fight.

And never was there any halt of soldiering or crying, even when Ireland had disappeared in the mist beyond the American horizon. So when the North called upon its newcomers to fight, Colonel Meagher, the new Finn mac Cumhail, raised his regiments in New York, and the Irish regiments from Massachusetts, Pennsylvania, New Jersey, and the United States regiments of Washington, and all joined together to form the Irish Brigade.

Then were the Fianna marching again to the lands of Badb, and my cursed brother with them.

And nothing will suit the Fianna so much but that they

be first and fiercest in the fight, and show the greatest valor and the least amount of pain.

> *So they rush from the revel to join the parade*
> *For the van is the right of the Irish Brigade.*

## 2

MARCH CAME IN my dreams like the soft wind that swiftly turns bitter, and I stared many a night at my candle in the small room I had at the top of the Shinny. Or I'd sit working over my lace, building and building the delicate net rope, and as my fingers worked their well-known stitches I'd close my eyes and see Mike, how he stepped so light along the camp's corduroy streets, how he ducked into a tent to join a game of cards and drink a round of oh-be-joyful moonshine, how he drilled with his fellows in the muddy meadow where the trees were felled all around for miles and miles, a forest of stumps the witnesses to Mike's training in war.

I'd see him shoulder a gun, and drop to his knee, and sight along the bayonet at the advancing lines. And I'd try to see the Confederate lines, how they would advance, but that was where my dreams could not go.

General Hooker, the third general to have command and charge of the Army of the Potomac, sat mumbling his pipestem and dreaming of Richmond, the rebel capital in Virginia. This, while General Lee jigged about Virginia and dreamed of his home in Arlington, across the Potomac from Washington, the Federal capital. How laughable to have two such generals, each wishing to be where the other was. Each commanded squadrons, regiments, brigades, corps, entire armies of Irish boys, for the Irish fought for the Confederacy, too, and faced the Irish of the North on fields like Fredericksburg.

At that battle, boys of the Union Irish Brigade, commanded by the second general, General Burnside, were mowed down by the Irish boys of the 24th Georgia, melting like snow upon the ground before the advance. How glorious, cried the generals, weeping with pride. See how the Irish fight! See how well they die! The fame of the Irish Brigade grew with each man lost, and was as wide as the sea and tall as the masts in Galway Bay by the end of the battle. What matter that the battle was such a catastrophe for the Federal troops that Burnside resigned his command and Lincoln put in Hooker? Glory was the Irish boys'.

It was at the Battle of Fredericksburg that Whitman's brother was wounded, and so brought Mr. Walt to Washington to meet me. Thus do all our dreams mingle and breathe together. Generals Hooker and Lee, Walt Whitman, the Fianna, Mike, and me, all dreaming and fighting together.

Hooker's devoutest dream, beyond Richmond, was more men, more men: Give me more men. Mr. Lincoln, give me more men so I may take Richmond and lay waste the rebel capital. And though Lincoln was dreaming of a general who would let Richmond starve to death and instead go after that dancing Lee, he gave Hooker more men.

" 'The Congress has passed the Conscription Act,' " read Finn from the newspaper at the Shinny on March 4. "They've done it now, and can draft anyone they like. Aliens exempt."

The fellows at the bar gave themselves winks of congratulation.

"I'll go if I like," Colm Peel declared in the thickest Dublin accent this side of the Atlantic. "But the draft board can go hang if they try to force me into the war."

"They'll draft aliens soon enough." Dooley looked sour. "S'long as this war goes on they'll be needing men."

"Yes, to replace the ones they've broken and can't play with anymore," muttered I to myself.

Milky Wesley was cradling Snatcher in his big hands. The terrier fixed me with a beady glance. "What d'you hear from your brother, Mairhe? Have they got him broken in yet?"

"Not a word, Milky, as you well know."

Milky included the other fellows in his knowing look. "No doubt he's liking it. That Mike is a natural soldier."

"Don't say so!" I whisked a half-empty glass out from under his nose, and left Wesley gaping dry as a fish and the dog flat-eared with surprise.

"Teach you to get on the wrong side of Mairhe Mehan," Dooley laughed. "Will you buy another, Milky?"

I stood by the window to steady my breathing, and

watched the twilight coming down. My fingers were idle and itched for the lace that was my constant occupation. Such yards I had, yet such spiderweb stuff it was. But it was making and it was holding together and it was twining and binding and I could see it. I could hold it and know I had fashioned it tight and strong and beautiful. The thread alone was so weak, so easy to snap. But when it was netted together with itself, oh, so strong it was!

But even as I turned to fetch my handwork there came a commotion and a clamor from outdoors, and I bent my gaze to see down the street. A riderless horse, harness flying, came trampling down our dead-end alley toward the Shinny, and a whole screaming crowd after it. The men in the bar yanked open the door and crowded together to see what the yelling was about.

The black horse was screaming and rearing, trying to find a way out of the box it was in, and the crowd of men and soldiers pressed forward, close to the flying hooves, and Snatcher darting back and forth all the while barking mad as a demon. All was dim and shadowy in the alley, but the sky above was still bright and clear, if the horse could only fly up to it.

"Get it, goddammit!" a fat and sweating sergeant yelled. "Control that beast, wrangler!"

A small man tried to duck in to grab the reins, but the horse was white-eyed and sidling and tossing about too wild to capture. The army wranglers were bringing horses from the West every day to break for cavalry mounts, and the barns all over Washington were filled with half-wild horses. I'd seen the wranglers breaking these horses in the big corrals, and seen a man trampled, but this was a first, an unbroken horse tearing up the alley outside the Shinny.

While the shouting and barking continued to lash the horse wilder, and the men from the Shinny laid bets on who'd get the best of the fight, the wrangler darted in again to grab the reins and took a hoof in the middle of his back. He went down under the hooves, and the sergeant whipped his hat off in fury.

"Control that animal or shoot it!" he screamed, pushing two soldiers forward. "Get that wrangler out and subdue the animal!"

The horse was dancing and shying and unwilling to step on the unconscious wrangler. As it backed into a corner the men in the doorway of the Shinny stepped out into the alley for a better look, leaving the door wide open.

And all in a flash the maddened horse lowered his head and bolted into the Shinny itself, crashing into tables and skidding in the sawdust of the wooden floor. Crockery and glass smashed all around it, and the men poured back inside in astonishment to see an unbroken horse break their saloon to bits.

"Get that thing out!" Dooley yelled, and Mrs. Dooley took one peek through the kitchen door and disappeared with a shriek.

The sergeant stepped in and shot the horse in the shoulder with his pistol. The animal screamed again and went down thrashing. Then the sergeant stepped closer and shot the creature between the eyes.

Then all was silence, but for Snatcher barking, barking at the dead animal's bleeding head in the smoky, rising dust.

## 3

WHAT WITH THE destruction and devastation of the furnishings of the place, and the blood and the dead horse in the middle of the wreckage, and all so appalled they had a dry and churchlike feeling of doom and left for home, Dooley was irate. Furthermore he forbade us to make any inroads in picking up the place, for he was determined to have compensation for his loss from the Army and make them dispose of the carcase, though Mr. O'Callahan was all for butchering it and Milky Wesley wanted it for dog's meat.

And so all cleared out before the barman's shouts of outrage, and the Dooleys and I sat in the kitchen in a dire silence, for the weight of the dead horse oppressed us all. Mrs. Dooley and I made a dinner of sorts, and Dooley muttered his anger into his plate and ticked off Quartermaster, Attorney-General, War Department on his thick fingers.

In the morning I found it had not been a dream, though I stepped into the saloon with a hope that it would be all as usual.

"Disgusting, I say," Mrs. Dooley said from the far door. She stood wringing her hands, sick to leave such a sight uncleaned. In the middle of the room lay the horse, and the bloody sawdust around it hard and dark.

"Get on, Mairhe," she added. "Dooley'll be all over the city today trying to get satisfaction of the government, which I doubt not he'll never see. Go see your Da, take him our love."

When I didn't move, she shooed me angrily away, and I stepped unwilling into the street.

A clear morning, and the smell of mud from the Tiber was ripe and mossy. I had not been to St. Aloysius to see my Da since he'd gone in on the church's charity, and I had no wish to do so now, so I turned myself toward the center of the city, looking for some sight that would cheer me more than a horse lying dead in a saloon. I knew I'd not find it watching a man fight against his own memories and dreams.

Well, there were those things about the day that could have brought me cheer. Early March it was, but there was a tenderness in the air. Folks were out walking, and though the city streets were rutted worse than ever with the artillery wagons and ambulances and all, the mud was soft and yielding, and not so cruel to the feet. One man called to another, and a mother called her son, and two small girls laughed on a doorstep as they scraped mud from their shoes. The stamp and jingle of horses drawing gigs down the avenues, and the squeal of a pig chased by boys, and cows lowing as a drover herded them along, and the ringing of a hammer from a smithy—these sounds all beckoned me forward in a daydream of the county fair of

Sligo, where Matthew Mehan would fight all comers in the ring.

And oh, couldn't I see it so plain, hear the bleating of sheep and smell the bay and see my father all in his prime, all in his prime. This loss of things, this angry breaking apart of what I loved and what was best around me, had plagued me all through the years. And at that moment it was so awful to me that I must stop and look at my own two hands. I must clutch my hands together and feel my fingers, to see that I myself was not falling into shards and fragments, or tearing down the things around me as I fell, as a tall tree falls in the forest and destroys the things around it.

But no, I was not broken, though I felt as slender and drawn as a thread.

A gig rattled by beside me in the street, startling me out of my dream. Still gripping and holding my own hands, I walked on. I walked on until I stood within sight of the Capitol, where all was building, building, building.

Can a person be two things at once? Can we believe in one thing strongly and equally in its opposite? Can we believe in union, and in independence as well? Can we be both American and not American, Irish and not Irish? Must we choose?

Whitman, now, that man could embrace in his big arms equally the Michigander and the Georgian, the man of Tennessee and the man of Massachusetts, the farmer of Carolina and the factory worker of New York, the wood-man, the shopgirl, father and brother—all things equally within him and he carried them all so light. Easy for him to say!

But I found myself all alone looking at the Capitol, not knowing what I was nor wanted to be.

# 4

SAINT PATRICK'S DAY, and wasn't there a wild Irish bang-up everywhere? The Shinny was restored, though Dooley himself had fallen into a black humor from which nothing could persuade him. Yet the saloon was thick with Irish folk, and music filled the air, and I feared I'd wear out my shoes from treading from bar to tables with dripping mugs of ale.

And there was a laughing, dancing, hand-clapping roar of the rollicking crowd at the Shinny, while in Kelly's Ford, Virginia, the Saint Patrick's festivities were of a different nature. There, three thousand Federal horse troops under W. W. Averell were riding to cross the Rappahannock for to engage the Confederates at Culpeper. The column of cavalry raised a fine dust in the spring air, and the dust settled on the blue shoulders and tilted blue hats of the riders. Blue jays carked and screeched between the trees at the jingle of the bits and the clank of sabers against stirrups and the clink of horseshoe on stone.

I say it was like the clank and clink of mug against mug as I set them down at the crowded tables, and the finest particles of sawdust from the floor drifting in among the

smoke, and one man called to another to take out his fiddle, 'twas time for a tune.

In the column a captain raised his hand, and the jog-
ging and jostling of horses came to a huddling halt behind
him. A horse snorted and tossed its head. One man
bethought himself of a pipe, and another man wondered
on the beautiful white arms and throat of his young wife
back with her family in Illinois, and yet another scratched
his chigger bites and looked across the ford into the far-
ther woods. The sun slanted down on Kelly's Ford, where
the Rappahannock sparkled and gleamed over the shal-
lows, and the mud along its bank held the dainty dancing
prints of raccoon and possum. The horses shifted from foot
to foot, smelling the water, and turned their ears one way
and another against the flies.

And so the men in the Shinny shifted their chairs
about, and a table or two was shoved aside to make room
for the dancing. Colm Peel took up a bow, and Finn took
a whistle from his pocket, while Milky Wesley began to
drum on a tabletop with a galloping beat.

The beat, so soft at first, was clearer to hear through the
woods whence Averell's cavalry came. The horses beneath
them were the first to be sure, for their ears pricked and
their necks arched, even as Averell gave the command to
wheel about and re-form with the ford at their backs. Up
the woodland road came the rebels, fierce as rebels, swearing to keep the Federals from crossing Kelly's Ford. Jeb
Stuart's dreaded Virginia Cavalry was riding to pound the
Federals.

And so it began, with Colm Peel taking the beat from Milky Wesley, and Finn joining a skirling little reel that ran above the fiddler's bow. Around them, the men clapped their hands and tapped their feet, and when the tune settled into one they all knew, didn't they sing? And didn't they dance and carry on, and the smoke and the kicked-up sawdust thicker and the clapping and stomping louder and louder by the minute, and even the fiddler whirling with the rest and the shouts and all mingling withal?

Limbs flying, mouths agape, bodies jerking this way and that—such noise and confusion was as natural to battle as the blood and the litter of cartridge boxes and dropped hats and dented canteens and dead men. The Union troops formed themselves around a small farm as the Confederates pressed them hard. Horses trampled new-furrowed fields, the flags were carried first here and then there, officers shouting from horseback and vaulting fences, the artillery bombardments raising fountains of dirt and stone, the wounded, crying men carried behind chicken coop and hog pen and springhouse. Shot horses kicked and struggled in bloody mud, and cries for water, please, water, as the sun heated the ground, rose like a groaning choir. A man, sitting foolishly in a mudhole, held his blasted hand in his other hand and looked up.

"Help me, Mairhe. Give me a hand."

Mrs. Dooley took me by the arm, and led me to the kitchen. "It's all I can do to lift this kettle of praties off the stove," said she.

I had a great urge to help her and return to the bar, and throw myself into the celebration with the others. For it is true that none can listen to Irish tunes without knowing she's Irish, and wanting to pound that truth into the floor with her feet. So I hurried after Mrs. Dooley, and we two dashed the praties from their boiling kettle, and then I was out again with the folks who had no part of America or its war in them.

"Give us a song I can do, Mr. Peel," I begged as I stepped near that man.

And he brought a cease-fire in a moment by raising both bow and fiddle in the air. "Boys, be still. Mairhe Mehan will favor us with a song."

" 'Nancy Whiskey'!"

" 'The Girls of Galway'!"

"Nay, make it 'A *Ghaoth Andeas!*' " I said.

The laughter stopped and Peel tapped the strings with his bow. " 'O South Wind!' "

With the men around me, and Peel and Finn to accompany me, I sang the Irish words, A *Connachta an tsóidh, an tsuilt is an spóirt, I nimirt is in n-ól an fhíona, Sin chugaibh mo phóg ar rith ins a' ród. Leigim le seól gaoith eí.* . . . Oh joyful Connacht, home of sport and wine, I send my kiss rushing down the road to you, I send it on the wings of the wind. I live in splendor, yet am I drawn home to you when I hear the music of the pipes.

The Gaelic was rough and salty in my mouth and the Shinny men sang tunefully with me as I closed my eyes tight and tried to dream of Ireland, tried to make it the dream of my heart and let the south wind blow me there.

But I couldn't, you see, for all I had of Ireland was dreams of it, and they weren't even my dreams to begin with. And when you have nothing at all, a dream will only lull you into dreaming forever.

That I would not do.

LINCOLN'S

HORNPIPE

# 1

HORNPIPE: A SOLO sailor's dance. Imagine a man kicking his heels first to one side and then the other as he squeezes and draws on the wheezing concertina, and there you have the very picture.

On a fine Saturday morning early in April, Mr. Lincoln made his gloomy, black, and stork-legged way to the Washington Navy Yard, there to board his little steamboat, the *Carrie Martin*. He stood at the prow as the boat chugged its way down the Potomac—a beak-nosed scarecrow of a figurehead, the light dappling up onto his dark face from the water—and folded his arms.

In this stance did he make his riverine way to see General Hooker at Fredericksburg, to see if he might persuade his commander to ask General Lee for a dance.

General McClellan had not engaged Lee and so General Burnside cut in. Yet General Burnside had not engaged Lee, and so General Hooker cut in. Now General Hooker, damnably, would not engage Lee!

"Forget Richmond," muttered the President under his breath as the banks of army-trampled Virginia farmland slipped past the *Carrie Martin*. "The enemy is not *at* Richmond, sir, but there, ahead of us."

The *pocka-pocka-pocka* of the little boat's steam engine caused the gray, beaky wading birds to fly up in a gawky confusion, flapping wide, ungainly wings from the muddy greenery at the river's edges, their long legs dangling behind them. Lincoln watched them, brooding, and again muttered in sardonic tones, "Forget Richmond, sir. Or if you will not use the Army, let me borrow it at least."

And one week later, back went the President, standing at the prow of the *Carrie Martin*, gloomier than ever, still dancing solo. *Pocka-pocka-pocka*. General Hooker would not engage General Lee. The South only survived because of Lee, and Hooker would not take him on.

In camp, Mike was cleaning his fingernails with a knife, and basking in the attention of questions that bombarded him. For the President had reviewed the troops while he was struggling to persuade Hooker, and Mike had let it be known that he was a Washington boy and had seen Lincoln many times, even stopped in at the President's House at a public reception or two. Mike's company was quartered near one from Wisconsin, and the Irish boyos were peeling money from the farm kids in poker.

"Sure, haven't I seen him riding to and fro the Soldiers' Home, where he spends the summer months?" Mike said, leaning back against a crate of ammunition. "Sits a horse about as well as a sack of praties does."

"D'you suppose he noticed us in the review?" asked Willie Arendt, the cards slack in his hands, and his mouth slack, too.

Mike caught a glimpse of Willie's deuces and treys and gave the boy a saintly smile. "Who could help noticing what a fine figure you are, Willie? Sure and the President was that impressed. Your worth is plain for all to see."

With that Mike put down his hand—full house, queen high—and picked up Willie's stake. Mike tossed the coins into the air and caught them as they fell.

Willie was dismayed, but never doubted Mike played straight. "Again? You've got some luck with cards, Mehan."

"I do, I do."

Donny Gallagher, Mike's mate, dragged his cap down over his mouth to stifle a laugh and stretched his feet in his too-tight boots. "He's a rare one, that's certain."

"Tell about Washington," begged another Wisconsin lad, named Johnny, whose hair was so blond it shone white in the dim of the tent.

Mike pretended to consider, and took a pull from his canteen. "It's a city that grabs a man—"

"Is that right?" Johnny asked.

"When he steps into the mud that's ankle-deep," Mike added, wiping his mouth on the back of his hand. "And never did you see such a collection of proud officers— leaning against the bar at Willard's Hotel."

"And girls. The Washington girls are pretty, isn't that so?" asked young Willie.

Mike's nimble fingers now made quick work with the cards. "The girls are sweet, I cannot tell a lie. And my sister the sweetest of all, for she wept a rain of tears when I left for the war."

"Proud of you, eh?"

"Not to say proud, no . . ." Mike drawled.

Willie nodded. "Fearful of your life, is that it?"

"To tell you the truth," and here Mike lowered his voice, and leaned forward so his hat tipped over one eye, "I believe she'd come track me down if she knew how to get a pass to cross the picket lines, and would march in here and take me home bodily to the bosom of my family. For we neither of us can write more than our names, you know, so she'd never try to persuade with a letter. But she wants me home, boys, I guarantee that."

Johnny slapped his knees. "Picture it, a girl coming down here to an army camp and trying to talk you into anything, Mike!"

"But his sister," Willie protested. "A fellow has to listen to his sister."

At that, Mike swept up the cards. "That's enough play, boys, I've got to see a man about a horse."

He stooped to leave the tent. Above his head, the clear sky blazed, and at his feet, the corduroy street of saplings laid side by side by side stretched at right angles through a city of dingy tents. Wherever he looked were regimental flags, state flags, the colors of all the troops of the great and stagnating Army of the Potomac. The stench of the latrines held away from him, and he breathed deep the smell of mud and bad coffee and damp clothes, and heard the sound of coughing rattle from one end of camp to another.

And did he wish his sister came? Did he give her a thought as he went down the street to the barbering tent for to get himself a shave? Or did he think only of army matters, that he'd go mad sitting in camp all spring, endlessly parading and drilling and marching in columns, walking picket lines, waiting for Hooker to make up his mind?

For if he could not fight, why was he here? If he could not prove himself an American by fighting, why should he stay?

# 2

SO AFTER ALL the grieving and despair I'd known, watching in silence while all around me fell to pieces and I not lifting a finger to stop them, then at last did I decide what course to take. A pass I must secure, an official pass from a military authority, an office of the government. The government was all around me, but I'd no more notion where to go than a cat does.

Thus it was that in my spare moments I took to haunting the hospitals in the last days of April, dancing from foot to foot, my hands clasped before me, or alternately caught behind my back. For I had my own hornpipe to dance, and wait through. And as the days increased in the spring, and the fruit sellers plied the avenues, and the salesmen hawked their patent medicines and five-cent books, I paced beneath the leafing trees outside one hospital and another, waiting for a glimpse of Mr. Walt.

And then, outside the Patent Office hospital one day, there he was, striding down the steps in a queer wide sombrero and a pair of cordovan boots, his shirt open at the throat like a stevedore's and his pockets stuffed and bulging.

I doubted he would remember me, but I knew of no one else close to the Army. I stepped out to meet him.

"Mairhe Mehan, is it?" said he.

"Yes, sir."

He beamed at me, his eyes bright behind his bushy beard. He smelled of coffee and bacon. "Come to work in the hospital, have you?"

I stepped backward so suddenly I nearly fell. "Sir, not at all, but to ask you for help."

"Well, then, walk with me down to Pennsylvania Avenue, as I have some commissions to carry out at the Capitol."

He set off, arms swinging, and I must hurry to catch him up.

"Mr. Walt, I need a pass to get me out of the city and conduct me across the picket lines at the army camp."

Just as suddenly as he started, he stopped, and looked at me keenly. "I don't take you for a camp follower, nor do you need a pass for that. So what's your business, Mairhe Mehan, and why do you think I can help you in it?"

An organ grinder began to play across the street, and the smell of roasting chestnuts came to me on the air as I waited for the heat to leave my face.

"This is the way of it. My brother's gone for a soldier, believing my father and me to provide for one another's comfort. But my father's mind broke down just as my brother left, and he has been taken in on charity, and I've no support but my brother. So I would go and tell him that, and have him return to Washington and save him from this war."

Mr. Walt took up his walking again. "And are you living on the streets, Mairhe, or on charity yourself?"

And then was I crying and could not help it. "Sir, I know I am poor and have no claim on you, but neither do I deserve that you always reproach me. It is true I live at the Shinny now, where I am the barmaid and so work for my place. But I feel every day the pain and the woe that this war is bringing. I feel it in my dreams at night and during the day. I can't hold so much misfortune in me without my brother to help me, and I know no one else I can ask for aid."

Mr. Walt dragged a handkerchief from his pocket, and handed it to me as we walked on. I wiped my face. It smelled of sweat and chloroform, and I knew he'd wiped soldiers' eyes and brows and cheeks with it and so it lapped my tears, too. A barouche rattled by on taut springs, a well-dressed lady inside. Mr. Walt stood to watch it go, and then did he give me a smile.

"I feel it too, Mairhe," said he at last. "I feel it every day and night, just as you do. That's why I go to the hospitals, and try to help those poor boys who suffer so much. I feel it does me some good to do them some good."

"Don't ask me to go into the hospitals," I begged. "I can't bear it."

"I believe you could."

I shook my head, and couldn't answer. We came abreast

of the organ grinder, who dolefully turned the crank of his organ and kept his eyes on the ground. Mr. Walt and I went on by him, and the mechanical tune faded behind us.

"I won't press you. Where's your father, now?"

"St. Aloysius, our church that now is an army hospital."

He nodded, and took off his sombrero to wipe his brow with his sleeve. "How is he?"

When I did not answer, Mr. Walt jammed his hat back on his head and took my arm. "Come on, girl."

And so he pulled me through the pretty April streets of Washington until they turned to the muddy April streets of Swampoodle and the clock tower of St. Aloysius rose before us. Ambulances and mortuary wagons came and went as always, for as the spring brought floods and mud and warmer weather, so it also brought skirmishes and casualties. Mr. Walt paused to let two stretcher-bearers carry their bloody load into the main door of the church, and then went in.

This left me displaced entirely. Here was I, in my own Swampoodle, on the outside of things and apart. Down the street came the sounds of hammering and sawing from a coffin-maker's shop. I stood in a shadow, and watched the ambulance men discharge their duty. Faint groans and cries came from the wagons; the sunlight was dazzling outdoors, but the open door of the church led into darkness, like a crypt. I watched each moaning, wounded soldier as he was carried from the bright day into the dark, and then, stepping out of the black entrance was Mr. Walt, and my Da.

Old he looked, old and broken as he'd never looked before. He followed meekly at Mr. Walt's side, blinking in the sun like a pale shadow of Mr. Walt, wondering and tipping his face up at the bright sky. My heart coiled within my breast.

"Oh, Da," I said, going forward.

"Is it Deirdre, then?"

"No, Da. Her daughter and yours. Mairhe." I put his hand to my face.

"Mairhe. Mairhe." Da turned his head as the stretcher-bearers passed by us. He frowned. "They bring these boys here every day, I don't understand it atall. This is a church. Have they no sense of holiness?"

"Da—"

"Mairhe, where's Mike? Where's your brother?"

"He's in the Army, Da, but I'm going to get him out. We need him, you and I, and I'm going to bring him back so we'll be a family again, and we'll go west, and we'll start new."

"Connacht is as west as you may get," Da said with a laugh. "You may get west of Sligo, but not by much. Are you saying we'll go to Connemara? The Mehans in Connemara, now there's something to think on."

I felt Mr. Walt's gaze on us so full of tender pity that I couldn't meet his eyes. Through the door of the church behind us came Father Wiget, squinting in the sunlight.

"Matthew, how do you like to see your daughter?" the chaplain asked.

"Father, I want you to have a word with my son,

Michael. He's about here somewhere, mark me. He never minds what I say, but he'll listen to you."

"Come along in, Matthew. He may be somewhere inside." Father Wiget, with one arm about my father's shoulders, led the way back into the darkness of the church.

Mr. Walt and I stood where we were, the hammering from the coffin-makers echoing in the street. The pounding of the hammers resounded from the walls and roof of the church, pouring down like a rain of hammering, as though St. Aloysius itself were being fashioned into a coffin and the lid being nailed down.

"You oughtn't have brought me."

"Maybe not. I make any number of blunders when I try to do good." Mr. Walt sighed.

I turned away, for to find my path to the Shinny. Mr. Walt called after me.

"I'll see what I can learn for you. Don't hope for too much."

I looked back briefly. "I never do."

# 3

IF I TELL you there was a box at the opera, with people seated within it, I may tell you where around the box those people sat and what they watched, and those are the facts of the case. But where's the truth of it? A man seated on a red chair across an uncrossable stretch of carpet from the red-haired woman he loves may be holding her hand in his heart. And although the woman in velvet who lifts the gilded opera glasses to her eyes and parts her lips sits beside her mother and even whispers kindly to her from time to time, she may be miles from her in spirit. And though the opera upon the stage may be found in the libretto, the opera each watches is a private affair.

Or I may tell you that the aeronauts ascended the sky in their delicate hot air balloons, and gazed far afield at the enemy army camps, and telegraphed their reports down the long, long wire to the ground. Ten units of cavalry here. One battalion deployed thus. The ground is level and open, rising to the west. But does the aeronaut's message contain the dismay he feels as he beholds the blasted woodlands to the south? And does he know that the man on the ground who decodes his telegram has three brothers in that army? And do they either one hear the voices of the men in that camp who clean their guns and write letters home, and slowly turn the pages of their Bibles?

So is history to be found in the heart and memory and the imagination, not in the photographer's glass plate or the journalist's wired message to the editor.

So these dreams are true, I tell you, as true as anything else.

And if I tell you I kept my brother alive by dreaming of him, that is true too.

How else could I fill the days of April, waiting to hear from Mr. Walt, waiting to know if I could go to my brother, if I could send to his commander and pull him from the ranks? I danced a perpetual hornpipe back and forth and back and forth in one place, waiting, waiting for the music to stop, making my lace without end, and wishing not to think of my Da.

So as the month drew to its close, and Lincoln proclaimed a national day of prayer for the restoration of the Union, I dreamed of the murmur of advance moving through camp like a wind moving through leaves, louder as it neared and growing more distinct. I dreamed Mike looking up from his cards, and giving grave Gallagher a glance.

"This is it, boys," Gallagher announced.

"How'd you know it?" Mike asked. He jerked a thumb out the tent. "Nothing but noise and shouting, so far."

A corporal leaned his head in under the canvas. "They're blowing assembly in a minute, lads. Strike camp. Looks like Lincoln finally lit a fire under Hooker's boots."

"Mother of God, it's about time, too," Mike swore, and rolled from his perch and landed on the ground. He grabbed up his hat and slapped it across one palm. "Let's go a-soldiering."

And out stepped Mike from under the shade of the mildewed canvas tent, into the April sunshine and mud of the camp. The quartermaster wagons were already rolling, the drovers whistling and whipping, and a mule bucking as it backed into its harness, and a brace of men putting their shoulders to the wheels of an artillery cannon to dislodge it from the mud, and a man emptying a coffeepot into a cook fire, and above the smell of army camp was a soft breeze blowing toward the Rappahannock and battle, boys, battle!

So rank and file assembled themselves into their units, and the flashy officers paraded on their arching horses, and the shouts of command passed from division commander to brigadier general to colonel to captain, and the soldiers all hearing the echoes not dwindling but growing louder and louder all about—forward!

"And if your sister could see you now?" Gallagher asked of Mike.

Mike patted the canteen at his hip, tested the straps of his rucksack, weighed his rifle. "If my dear sister could see me now, she'd be carping and complaining on something, I promise you that. For she's always in a black mood and wouldn't see the joy of this moment."

With a squint around at the marching mass, Gallagher spit into the mud, which was a good mud, soft underfoot but not so deep the wagons would roll it to ankle-turning ruts. "Does she not appreciate what we're fighting for?"

"What we're fighting for," Mike repeated, eyes ahead on the marching blue backs. "What we're fighting for . . . No, by God, she does not."

# 4

MR. WALT CAME into the Shinny, breathless and with biscuit crumbs in his beard. "Mairhe, I have been much about on this business of yours and I may have some hope for you."

I poured him a glass of beer and set it before him careful and slow. "Tell me."

"I've done a good amount of clerking at the Paymaster General's office—it's how I earn my room and board—and I put your case to a friend of mine there. He arranged for you to go with me to the War Department to plead your case and see if we can't get your brother discharged."

I stared at his face, watching him speak these words.

"Now, Mairhe. Come now."

And without further fuss or falter, we went out the door making for the War Department at Pennsylvania Avenue and Seventeenth Street. I didn't say a word as we hurried along, didn't answer as Mr. Walt pointed out the tender lilacs blooming in a dooryard or called to my ear the queer high calls of the drovers as they yipped and hied a herd of cattle onto the lawn of the President's House. My thoughts were of Mike only, and of getting him out.

So Mr. Walt understood me and ceased calling my attention to this spring herald or that, and only led the way to the office where we were to go. Artillery cannon flanked the building, and soldiers guarded the door. We went into a moving mass of blue uniforms and the high echoing confusion of men's voices filling the high hall and the tramping of feet. Mr. Walt tucked my hand firm under his arm, and in his easy way asked to make way, and conveyed us through the voiceful clamorous crowd to an officer seated at a desk, beset on all sides by soldiers and officers and aides.

"Not now, goddammit," the officer said, brushing aside a sheaf of papers thrust before him and resuming his parley with a beefy man in a stained uniform. "—Chancellorsville, that area, find the appropriate maps to take to the Secretary's office—"

We stood before him, waiting to be noticed. Mr. Walt was still and silent, his white-haired, white-bearded, white-shirted figure standing out against the dark blue sea like a lighthouse.

"Yes, what is it?" the officer asked abruptly. "This isn't the right place for casualty lists, you know."

"Where do we find Major Hanford?" Mr. Walt asked.

The officer pointed, relieved to be rid of us so easily. "Third floor, that way. No, not now," he snapped again at an aide at his side.

We went up the right-hand stairs that echoed with bootheels and military mutterings and the jingle of cavalry spurs. The place was a murmurous mass, active as a kicked-over anthill. The uniformed officers and soldiers gave us only hurried passing glances as we went up: the white-haired bearish man, and me, a black-haired Irish girl with dark eyes large and staring.

At the landing, two officers with gold braid stood in silhouette at the window, the bars outside the glass cutting them into pieces like stained glass. They looked up as we came, and one drew the white gloves from his belt and ran them through his hand, and then inclined his head to his fellow officer and looked at us not again. We turned onto the next flight up. My heart was pounding. The staircase switched back and forth as it climbed, and men continually bore down on us as we battled upstream against the current.

"Don't be frightened, Mairhe," Mr. Walt said, wondering around at the noise and frantic action. "Your petition will be heard."

When at last we reached the proper floor, he led me by the hand down the corridor. Oaken doors loomed beside us, and opened here and there or shut abruptly. Aides with papers and dispatch cases went in and out.

"Is it always so—so all of a frenzy?" I whispered.

Mr. Walt looked cautiously around, and bent his head down to mine. "Something may be happening soon. I don't know— Ah, here we are."

He pulled me along, and I followed through the door into an office. The appointments were richer than any I'd ever seen, the polished desks, the silk flag, the Turkey carpet on the floor. Mr. Walt beckoned to me where I stood like a statue.

"Now, Miss Mehan," spoke the man at a desk, this Major Hanford. He didn't look up at me, but at the paper before him. His fingers were ink-stained, his desk littered with dispatches and lists and ledgers. "What is the nature of your petition? I have your brother's name and his regiment before me. What is it you wish to ask?"

"He's gone away into the Army thinking my Da and I'd look out for each other—"

"And?"

"And my Da took ill and is taken into the parish on charity, sir, and I am on my own. I've no other family."

Major Hanford looked up. Light from the window put a sheen on his sandy hair and mustache, but did nothing to light his eyes. "Was your brother a conscript?"

I clutched my hands. "No, sir, he's Irish. Exempt from the draft, sir. He enlisted in January."

"Hmm. If he'd been drafted that would be one thing. But if he chose to enlist—"

"But sir, he didn't know how he'd be leaving me," I whispered. "Didn't know what his leaving would do to our Da. He wouldn't have signed on if he knew."

The sound of tramping feet grew loud in the hallway, passed the door, and grew faint. I saw Mike walking away from my Da, and my Da putting his fist through a window, and all the time Mike knowing what he'd done to us. And then I knew he'd broken my heart as carelessly as he'd broken anything else.

Around me, the edges of my vision began to fade.

"What's wrong with the girl?"

"She looks faint."

"Can't you do something?"

"I'm well enough," I said. I gripped the edges of the polished desk, and my fingers left smears. I noticed the officer noticing them.

"Yes, well, let me look into this matter," he said, tapping some papers together. He didn't look at me. "Come back in . . . shall we say ten days."

"Ten days?"

"There are many cases to be reviewed, Miss Mehan. Yours will receive its attention in its time. And it happens this is a particularly bad time to be asking."

"The Army's advancing?" Mr. Walt asked, keening forward.

"Good day to you."

"Sir? Will you get him out?"

Mr. Walt took my arm and led me out of the room. "We can only ask so much at one time."

Out in the hall I stopped and looked up at him. I could feel tears in my eyes. "Why'd he do it to me?"

"The Army has these regulations—" Mr. Walt began.

"Oh, wirra, wirra! No." I shook my head and went blindly for the stairs. "No."

He fell into step beside me. I ducked my face away, but he was a man who knew weeping when he saw it, silent or no. He walked ahead of me, and the blue resonating crowds parted around us and closed behind us as water closes around a moving bubble, until we came out into the sunshine of the avenue.

"What is it, Mairhe? What's happened?"

I put one hand to shield my eyes, and dropped my head for I couldn't bear it that my brother had done this to me, left me with nothing at all to dream of.

"My brother knew what he was doing," I said in a dull voice. A soldier brushed my shoulder in passing, knocking me aside. "He knew what he was doing and didn't care."

"Perhaps he didn't know. If he loves you, he wouldn't have done it."

I looked up at Mr. Walt. "Ah, but that's it, isn't it? And if he doesn't love me, what have I got? Not a thing in this world."

"You've got your country," he solemnly said.

"Jesus and Mary, you don't understand it at all, do you! I haven't got any damned country, have I? I don't belong to anyone or anything or anyplace. If I am divided from my brother, I am in pieces. I am a fragment. I have no more substance than a dream that's gone."

Mr. Walt stood there like a rock, like a tree, like a house, just looking and looking at me until I was so angry I hit him in the arm. And again he only looked at me, so I walked away from him, back to Swampoodle, the Irish bog that I called home, there to close my eyes to what I'd seen and keep my dreaming deep.

For what could I have known of that furor and frantic flow of men and officers within the War Department? What could I have known but what I dreamed of my brother, as his regiment moved up the Virginia road to Chancellorsville, which was nothing more than a single grand house, and removed the rebuking Chancellor women who defied them from the colonnaded porch?

And General Hooker made the place his headquarters, there to wait for Lee in the open ground, at the advantage. A hundred and thirty thousand men of the Army of the Potomac, invincible, unmovable, thick on the ground in their legions, waiting for Lee's small barefoot and butternut army to fall before them. They could not lose. The time was come to crush the foe, to salt his wells, and put his face in the dust.

And when the battle began it wasn't one battle but many over the first budding days of May, in the primrose woods and on the buttercup hilltops, with cavalry and entrenchments and gun-smoking moonlight and Hooker incredibly giving up the advantage at every turn, and Lee continually dividing and dividing again his small forces to shatter Hooker.

Mike sat with his comrades at a fire as the sun rose on the second day of battle, cooking coffee on the misty ground and marveling that they were alive, and a fox sprang out of the thicket and ran straight through their fire, scattering sparks as red as its tail and upsetting the coffeepot into the flames with a hiss.

And the first thought was to give chase, have a merry fox hunt in the morning fog, albeit without horse or hound, when stumbling after the fox in all their hurry and surprise and mortification was a unit of the North Carolinas still lost at the end of the long and shot-filled night, as much dismayed as the Federals were to have gotten so lost in the confusion and so waylaid by the smell of coffee.

All the men stood aghast and unready in the moving cloud of mist and smoke, some with steaming cups, some with rifles. Mike had time to notice the rent at the knee of one Carolina boy's trousers, and the freckles that ran over his nose, had time to observe that everything was gray and brown in the mist, like the figures in photographs, that they all stood as still as the figures in photographs, posed with their weapons and their cocked hats and their startled staring faces. The only color was the red glow of the fire, and the red memory of the red fox like a splash of blood across the clearing.

Then to the left through the trees came the renewed boom of artillery, and bugle calls, and without a word the photographs dissolved and no one who had been there was there, and Mike was running back to where he'd left the Chancellor House.

It was battle he was in, the Lands of Badb, more confusing and disorderly than he'd ever thought, officers screaming orders none could follow, dead mules lying in the road, a dead horse *smoldering*, for God's sake, the bombarded topless trees like giant tombstones in the pale moving mist, the tang of gunpowder sharp as a bayonet in his throat, and up ahead, there was that stately building, broad and dignified, its ranked columns white in the mist. And to Mike the pale white glow of the sun rising behind it put a dome on the roof.

Then a cannonade bloomed behind him, knocking him forward in a hail of dust. He stumbled, his eyes on the house looming before him that looked, to his closing eyes, like the Capitol. And, "Jesus, Mairhe," thought he as he fell, "what have I done?"

"HOLY GOD, IT'S a bloodbath," Dooley moaned, all dismayed.

The faces around Finn with the newspaper were grim and grave, for none could believe that bloody eejit Hooker had actually lost. Lost! With superior arms and armies he had lost against Lee.

"Lincoln will eat him for supper," Finn said, turning the cheap pages with fingers black with newsprint. "But none of our boys in the casualty lists, thank the devil. D'you suppose your brother was in the fighting at all, Mairhe?"

"He's all right," said I. "I'm going to get him out before the next big battle. He wants out. Mark me."

"Mark her?" O'Callahan quirked a brow. "What d'you know about getting a man sprung from the Army's clutches?"

I cleared dishes into a basin. "I know what I know. He enlisted, he can get out if he wants."

"Mairhe," Dooley warned. "He enlisted, and that means he wants to fight."

"I will get him out, I say. I've an appointment to do so."

"And why'd you say he wants out, Mairhe? Tell us that?"

"I know what I know!"

The men at the Shinny passed a doubtful look around, but I didn't heed it. I'd not give up the only dream I had. I'd no other way to survive the worst thing that ever befell me.

"But Mairhe, this looks like an earnest offensive, now, and the Army will follow Lee—"

"I won't hear it!"

While the Shinny men pored over the casualty lists in the paper, I ran back through the kitchen to the alley for air. I didn't stop there but kept running on out into the main streets into the steady traffic of ambulances. I walked the side of the street, head down to pick my way across the planks that crossed the worst mud, and always at my shoulder, at the corner of my eye, were the wagons of wounded rolling through the streets from the steamer landings on the Potomac to the city hospitals. The air about me was filled with groans and cries for help, for water, for a doctor, for mother, and as the wagons lurched in the rutted road the screams would peak into such a weight of sound that it pressed down upon me ever harder until I broke anew into a run.

And when I raised my eyes, there in an open square was a great mortuary tent before me. I knew what it was, for the smell of the embalming cut through every other smell there ever was. The wagons and bearers that milled about that tent were dreadful to see, like flies swarming a dead cat in the gutter, and Capital Police holding back shrieking crowds of citizens in search of their boys. It was grotesque. This was what Hooker had done with the Army of the Potomac, turned it into so many wagons of customers for the mortuary men.

I knew Lincoln must be still at his hornpipe, striding down to his steamer and making his way up the Potomac

to Hooker—who was retreating! Retreating in blockhead-
ed confusion and still muttering about Richmond. And I
on Lincoln's heels was busy with my own hornpipe, back
and forth, skipping up and down with my hands crossed
helpless behind me.

To the War Department I would go, and go again, and
every day until I could secure my brother's discharge. He
was an Irish boy, an alien, and had no business being in
the war, and I told myself this as I ran through the crowded nurse-milling, ambulance-rattling streets. I told myself
this as I made myself go up the steps full of officers and agi-
tation, I told myself this as I closed my ears to the curses
of men who told me to come back another time, didn't I
know there'd just been a military calamity? until I was
before Major Hanford and he looked up with pale blank
eyes and spoke to me:

"Today the President has signed the Alien Conscription Act. Your brother would be drafted and bound to
go now even if he hadn't already signed up. Of course, if
you can find three hundred dollars for a substitute, and
return the hundred-dollar bounty he took for signing up,
you can buy him out. But I don't suppose an Irish girl like
yourself can manage that sum?" He tapped his papers
together.

"I thank you, sir. Where shall I bring the money whenever I've got it?"

Major Hanford laughed through his nose. "Oh, come
back here and I'll tell you what to do with it. If you get it."

And with never giving him the satisfaction of making a

poor Irish girl weep, I left his office and fought my way down the crowded stairs. My hands were cold as winter's ice, and my mind was a confusion of trying to clutch at so many threads at once. Four hundred dollars! Holy God, what a fortune!

But I could earn money. I had lace. I could make more. I could cast it as a net to bring Mike back in, as a lifeline, as reins. With one thread I could save my brother.

And so did I dance faster and faster, all alone to save his life. I was a spider, I was a spinner, I was the ropemaker's mother and the weaver's daughter, I was the weaverbird and the silkworm, plying thread to thread. I was the kite flyer and the fisherman, pulling out the thread to pull my brother in with. The lace pooled about my feet.

When I dreamed my brother marching in April, I wove him a banner to follow home. When I dreamed my brother lifting a wounded friend in May, I wove him a bandage to hold back the blood. When I dreamed my brother swimming in the hot June, I wove a net to bring him back to land.

And all the while was Lincoln dancing faster and faster too, back and forth, up and down the Potomac on his little steamer to confer with disgraced Hooker and say: Do you see that Lee is invading the North, sir? Do you see what the rebel is doing? Will you not take this army I have given you and *fight* against him, sir?

Hooker, still addled from Chancellorsville, could not attack the rebel general, but wondered to Lincoln if he shouldn't instead invade Richmond. The music came faster and faster at this point, and Lincoln was dancing aboard the *Carrie Martin* like the maddest sailor ever was. Then at last did Lincoln replace General Hooker with General Meade, and then his hornpipe was done.

Meade led the army to chase after Lee. The rebs were in Pennsylvania, where there lay a town called Gettysburg, and it was all woe to me then. For my hornpipe wasn't over yet.

# 6

I DREAMED I was an old, old woman, that my sight was dim and my hands spotted brown and knotted with veins. My voice shook like water shakes when the cold wind blows across it, my back was as bent as a mountain, and my hair as white as a dead moth's wing. All alone I sat in a chair in a darkened room, and the world was dark around me, and my age was upon me like a heavy, hurting cloak, but all sounds were present and strong as I tipped my paper ear to the world.

I heard the sound of men laughing before battle.

I heard the sound of blood dripping into a pan, and a doctor's footsteps walking away.

I heard the sound of paper tearing, a mother opening the letter that bears news of her son's death.

And I rocked and rocked in my chair all alone, hearing the three sounds of sorrow.

# 7

THIS IS THE way it happened on July 1, 1863, or so the story goes:

Rebel soldiers, having trudged all the way up into Pennsylvania from their bean farms and their turpentine stills and their slow-river piers, and having had poor equipment to begin with (having but an impromptu government to support them), were marching on bloody feet. The ragged hems of their butternut britches licked their bare ankles. Their toenails were blackened with Maryland mud that caked and hardened on the hot summer road.

But there were shoes, someone said, shoes in the town of Gettysburg. And so the rebs turned back south down Cashtown Road in the heat, while the Feds were coming up north in the heat, and when they ran into one another, didn't the town begin to cook? Couriers and outriders boiled back through their own forces sending word, sending for support even as the artillery were hurriedly trundled and rolled into position and the officers in the rear were standing in their stirrups and straining through their field glasses and asking—What the hell is going on up there?

For none of them had known precisely where the other was, for to be sure, America is a big country, big enough for two big armies to lose one another in. And the weather was hot, and the men were dreaming of their hometown holidays upcoming, the Fourth of July picnics and horse races, the boating parties and the berry pies, the watermelons and chicken, the peaches warm from the sunny tree, and the sweethearts sitting under a sunny tree.

And God, weren't they tired, and weren't their feet sore and their legs aching? And their bellies not full enough with bad spoiled food, and their eyes not rested enough with bad spoiled sleep? But to hell with it all, for the enemy was there, and fight they must, for the shells were already pounding the ground and shaking the bricks from the houses, and the townfolk of Gettysburg rushing about and gathering up their scattered children and dogs and leaving their pickling half done on the kitchen table, the jars still tapping together as they boiled in the kettle.

And Mike was there, wasn't he?

Washington City was beside itself with the fear and the fury, the fighting truly north of us now and the rebels on Northern ground. We in the Shinny that July 2 and 3 sat waiting for each new edition of the newspaper through the evening, and Finn, or O'Callahan, or Dooley, or anyone with reading would read it. We stood gathered at the bar, our glasses untouched and growing warm in our hands, the heat heavy upon us and our heads aching with the heat and the worry of it all.

And as I heard the reports of the fighting on Little Round Top, Cemetery Ridge, and the Peach Orchard, Mike leaned back against a tree, wiping his smoke-black face on his sleeve and fixing his bayonet, his eyes white in his blackened face. The pounding of shells scarce made him flinch, for it was the regular sound of a beating heart, the sound of a hundred and fifty thousand beating hearts beating in time.

His company was gathered in the woods to the south of town, each man readying for the next attack. Some squatted on their heels, others leaned on their elbows or stood against the humid trees. Some men checked and rechecked their ammunition, fingering the bullets in their cases and squinting downhill through the tattered leaves. Other men wrote hasty notes to their wives or mothers and passed them to the captain. Some only stared dreaming into space, and the sound of their dreaming was the sound of water running over the stones in the near creek, and the low laugh of a man to his friend, and the murmur of prayer from another.

"Gallagher, give us your canteen, I'm dry as dust," Mike said.

Gallagher slung it off his shoulder, and passed it. The distant sound of rebel yells came to them like birdsong as Mike drank.

"Gives me a right uneasy sensation, how they scream," Gallagher said. He tried to spit but couldn't. "God, I'd like to be back in Ireland now."

"Would you? I wouldn't."

"P'raps you don't remember, then, what a lovely place it is," Gallagher replied.

Mike tossed the canteen to his friend, and tipped his head back to see the reddening sky through the mingling, croosheening leaves.

"I remember it."

He thought to say more, but didn't speak aloud, for his ears were filled with the sounds he wanted to hear: of waves on rocks and sheep bleating across the valleys, of spades turning wet earth and salmon thrashing up a stream, of a bagpipe's drone and a linnet's sweet call, and the sound of a woman washing clothes in a river. A sound of Ireland was in his ears.

"I remember it," he said again. "But I wouldn't go back. I choose America. It's good here."

And I bowed my head to the bar, all a wasteland in my heart. How could he say it? All he'd ever known was Swampoodle, the capital's slum, the hot, fumy slum at the heart of America. Here where it was hot, and the mud was thick and stinking, and we'd known nothing but trouble all our days since reaching this place. How could he say he chose America? What had it shown him but how to soldier on a hot road?

"Jesus, it's hot, isn't it?" O'Callahan complained. He ran a finger under his collar and drained his glass. "Well, good night to you all gathered here."

"Go to bed, Mairhe, you're done in," Mrs. Dooley said. She laid a hand on my forehead, palm down, then back down, and brushed the hair back from my face.

I pushed myself away from the bar, pushed myself up the stairs and to my room at the top of the Shinny, there to fall on my bed into a dreamless sleep.

I wakened in the dark.

There were no dreams.

There was no dream of my brother but the sound of a

gunshot fading from my mind. My dreaming had failed.

I shook the matches at my bedside, and scraped one alight. The corners of my room rose from the darkness, the rocking chair, the foot of my bed, the blanket box, and everywhere, on every surface and in baskets on the floor, lay the round wound balls of my lace, yards upon yards of it, stacked like bone-white cannonballs, like balls of ice, trailing their sad raveling ends.

How had I thought to weave a mile of lace? What was I thinking? I could not make things so by saying so, I could not spin a story and say it was the truth, I could not weave my way to my brother, I could not rope him like a horse and make him not be what he was. If I'd had all the money in the world, I could never have bought my brother out of the Army, for he had chosen to give his fighting heart to America.

I stood from my bed and reached for one end of lace, letting the ball drop and unwind, and draped the film about my shoulders and hair even as I grabbed another ball. And that fell too, to unroll on the floor as I wrapped myself in my own net, and another fell and another, and I turned and turned within my web, my shift white, my skin white, my hair as black as night, wrapped in the white, white web. I'd caught no one but myself.

The lace was good for nothing but bandages and winding cloths now. My brother was no more.

## 8

THE FOURTH OF July 1863 was celebrated throughout Washington. The cries and cheers and whoops of joy echoed from every building: Lee is whipped and on the run!

What mattered that the wounded from the first day of battle at Gettysburg were already rolling into the city at the train depots, the wagons howling with pain in the heat? What mattered that the men struggling in on their own feet looked like dead souls walking the streets? Women rushed from their doors with glasses of lemonade and plates of cake to feed the walking ghosts. At last, a glorious Union victory. Lee was whipped and on the run.

What mattered that the casualty lists, the printers' ink still wet and smearing like blood on the hands, bore the names of entire companies, whole regiments, the populations of towns? What mattered that fifty thousand names were on those lists? Lee was whipped and on the run.

Mrs. Dooley sat me down when Mike's name was read from the sheet at the Shinny, and wrapped my hands around a mug of tea.

"There, acushla, cry on me." She rocked me against her breast and crooned a keening cradle song, though I didn't cry. I didn't cry.

"I wasn't there," I told her.

"No, of course you weren't."

"I wasn't with him."

Mrs. Dooley smoothed my hair. "No, how could you be?"

"I'm all in pieces, how'll I ever put myself together again?"

"What are you saying, acushla, my girl? Don't talk so."

I stared over Mrs. Dooley's broad shoulder, to see the Shinny boys standing around with nothing to say. None would meet my eyes, none would speak. Milky stroked Snatcher's fist-sized head, and Finn slowly shook his head, and Dooley put his head on his hands and sighed.

"Raise a glass now, boys," said O'Callahan, and cleared his throat. "To Michael Mehan. *Slainte*."

"*Slainte*," said they all together.

And I opened the door and went out in search of my brother's death.

I staggered along the streets as stricken as the walking soldiers, and walked staring and stumbling down one street and then another until I was on North Capitol Street, and heading down it in the stream of ambulances, nurses, and wagons toward the Capitol. And there, as in a dream, I found Mr. Walt waiting for me on the steps, and he led me up into the building that was a hospital today, as every building was.

Before my eyes in the Rotunda stretched row upon row of white cots, like snow-covered graves in a frosted boneyard, but gaudy with living blood. Above the cots keened the mingling, croosheening wails of the men, all undone and doomed, and echoing in the dome above.

"Come on, girl." Mr. Walt stepped all large and delicate to the first blood-dripping bed, and there kissed a cheek.

"How are you, son?"

The red-haired soldier there gripped Mr. Walt's hand hard. His back arched. Above where his knees should have been was a spreading stain. "My sister's come, Doctor?" His voice was an Irish voice that made my heart faint. And then his back arched again and his cry of *"Ochone! Ochone!"* went through and through me like a cold red wind. Mike! Mike! Where is my brother?

"Your sister's here, son," Mr. Walt said to the raving man. "She's just arrived."

Mr. Whitman, the wildest largest-hearted dreamer of all, pointed and pointed at me until I *was* the man's sister and knelt by the bed and took the man's hot hand in my own.

"Sal? Is it you?"

"Here, macushla, m'darling," said I.

"Tell Ma I was brave," the soldier whispered to me.

"I will, macushla."

His eyes stared up. The red hair curled back from his brow, and a powder burn on his right cheek was wet and black. "And that I killed my share of rebs."

"I told her already, and she was glad to hear it but wants her boy home again. We sat last night over our sewing and spoke of our old times."

"And old Bren, he was there, Sal?"

"Sure. And we drank a health to you. *'Slainte!'* we said as we raised our glasses to you and called you our brave abu, our hero. And then one by one our neighbors stopped to drink *slainte* to you too."

"Not the MacReadys? They were never there too?" The man laughed, and stared hard at me.

I shrugged. "Sure and who but them? Didn't they always mean you well no matter what devil you did them?"

He laughed again and then cried again *"Ochone!"* And the red stain on his cover bloomed like a sudden rose and he died.

God send his spirit a dream of going home, a dream of stepping whole from the train in his Philadelphia, or his Trenton or his Albany, and seizing his laughing Ma in his arms and dancing her around. And she laughing and scolding and calling him her wicked spalpeen, her rascally rogue. Never would he have to say what house on the battlefield received him, what staircase running red he was carried up by the staggering stretcher men. There, where the fainting nurses bored holes in the floor to let the blood run out, where the surgeons carried their terrible saws from one man to another and parted man from limb— there was he parted from his dreams forever more.

"Mairhe," Mr. Walt said.

He took my hand to help me up, and we pulled the sheet over the soldier's face.

"I'll not see my brother again but in my own dreams."

"I think that's true, dear."

Mr. Walt moved down the ward, and was soon helping a nurse with a grisly chore. I stood over the shrouded soldier, and looked from him to the next and the next and the next, stretching away into the dimness. If I had my lace, I could join them one to another, bandaging their wounds with my work and binding their torn selves together.

I put my hand on the Irish soldier's head.

"Good-bye, macushla. Michael Mehan, good-bye."

Above my head was the old Capitol dome, round and fragile as the inside of an egg. And above that I knew to be the forming frame of the new dome stretching taller and reaching higher than ever before.

Would that old egg crack, and the broken boys down here be born from it and into the new? Did the Republic that labored so hard now plan to bring these boys with it? I strained to see upward in the poor light, up there where the mingling groans of the wounded soldiers resounded together, and I thought I heard the crack, so faint, only a crack.

THREE
BRIGHTNESSES
THAT
GIVE
HOPE
IN
TROUBLED
TIMES

# 1

WHEN THE LONG day was over, and the parades of Independence Day were but echoes in our ears, I went down the steps of the Capitol. Below me on the lower stone steps was a seated figure, with a broad back and white hair, and I went to join him where it was cool in the twilight. Mr. Walt was bent close over one of his small notebooks, writing in it in pencil. I looked out on the Capitol grounds, where the statue for the top of the building lay in pieces, waiting its chance to ascend the dome. It put me in mind of the tower of St. Aloysius, and my Da, and how I'd have to tell him about Mike.

"I'd like to get my Da back to Ireland," I told Mr. Walt.

He looked up at me sideways, all weariness and care on his face. Or it may be it was only darkness. "Why is that?"

"He never liked it here. Never got over my Ma's dying, nor got over leaving home. Ireland's his all."

"Ah." Mr. Walt planted his elbows on his knees. "I know that emotion myself."

"And he might return to himself once he's back where he belongs."

"That may be. That may be. And where do you belong, Mairhe?"

"I don't know. I used to belong where my brother was, but not now."

"Can't you belong where Mairhe Mehan belongs?"

I didn't have an answer for him. I touched the notebook that gleamed faintly white in the fading light. "Why d'you always carry these about and write in them?"

"Oh, I make memoranda in them," he replied, turning the pages with his thumb. "What the boys want me to bring them, what letters to write for them. I describe what I see, my observations."

"What for?"

"For poems, Mairhe."

I was surprised. "Are you a poet, then, Mr. Walt?"

He pulled his beard. "I'm known for one or two small things."

"Not Irish, are you?"

"No, not Irish, Mairhe."

A company of soldiers marched past us where we sat on the steps in the gathering dark. The air was warm and damp, and in the distance was the sound of fireworks, perhaps gunshots— I think fireworks.

"Will you tell me a poem, then, Mr. Walt?"

"They're long things, mostly. Pages and pages."

"Give us a piece, then."

He turned to look up at me on my step, and he put his hand on mine. "Very well. Here's a piece for you: 'Listen dear son—listen America, daughter or son, It is a painful thing to love a man or woman to excess, and yet it satisfies, it is great, But there is something else very great, it makes the whole coincide, It, magnificent, beyond materials, with continuous hands sweeps and provides for all.' "

His face was obscure in the dark, but his white hair shone brightly, like a cloud after the sun has gone down.

"What does it mean?"

He stood up. "It will be plain to you soon enough, I hope."

And so he went down the steps and walked away from me, a poet with bright white hair. He disappeared into the darkness of the war-struck city, but his hair remained visible, a halo about his head, for a long, long time. And I, watching him, felt a restfulness occupy my heart.

At last I took myself off, and made my way back to Swampoodle and the Shinny. Along the way I saw a glimpse through a window here, and a view through an open door there, the people laughing and toasting one another for Independence Day and the great Union victory, or reclining on the front steps with a harmonica and loved ones singing, and all around the city an easeful, peaceful joy that the chance of union was yet preserved to us.

I walked among the Americans like a shadow of myself, and when I reached the thrown light of an open door, I stood in it and raised my face to the house where there was music from a piano and a noisy, puppyish chorus of "The Battle Hymn of the Republic." And laughter came with the music, and high girl voices and a father's low rumble, and a woman came to the front door in a blue dress, looking back over her shoulder as she came and speaking to the inside of the house where the gaslight burned bright in the wallpapered hall.

Then she turned to shut the door and saw me standing there in the light at the bottom of her steps, and she smiled at me.

"Happy Fourth of July," said she as she made to shut the door.

"Same to you, missus," said I.

She paused, and looked at me kindly. "What's your name?"

I wove my fingers together. *Mary*, I wanted to say. *Mary*. But I hesitated too long, and with another smile she nodded and said, "Well, good night, then."

So I took the crooked ways and the narrow ways to the Shinny, and when I walked in, all was strange to me though so familiar: O'Callahan and Finn arguing over a newspaper, Leary and Dooley leaning across the bar toward one another to share some wisdom, Milky feeding Snatcher sausage scraps from his plate, and all the other men with their old clothes and their new opinions, with Mrs. Dooley moving big and homely among them. I knew them all, but in a day they had become distant from me, and their voices foreign to my ear.

As I entered, first one man and then another noticed me, and gave me a nod or a smile, and Mrs. Dooley whispered to me that I should eat something, and then go upstairs, and not to bother with work at all for couldn't I see she could manage, poor lovey? And I embraced her kind self hard, and went away from them all to my room.

Their Irish voices murmured me to sleep.

## 2

I DREAMED I was on a ship, and the ship was bound for Galway. I leaned my elbows on the taffrail and looked over the stern at the waves racing beside us in our wake, how they spun white lace at their tops and dissolved on the blacky deep, and above my head the shrouds and rigging wove themselves together like lace against the sky. And the salt spray of the waves was cool on my face, and the warm wind was on my hair. My hands were empty.

But then I knew I'd gotten on the wrong ship, and looked around me for the captain or the pilot, for to beg them to change the course. Above me in the shrouds not a sailor stirred, no helmsman took the helm, nor was there another soul on the ship.

I ran to the bow, and looked down into the leaping waters that rose and fell away as the ship plunged ahead. The only sounds were the thump and clack of block and tackle against the masts, and the sigh and breath of the rigging, and the ship's bell telling, and the snap of the sails as the wind pushed me forward toward Ireland.

So did I look about me, and know there was none to help me. I looked forward again, where the bowsprit pointed like my own arm pointing ahead across the wide Atlantic.

And then of my own will standing in the bow did I turn the ship and turn the ship, until the bowsprit pointed back toward America.

## 3

IN THE MORNING, I gathered my lace together, great bags of it neatly rolled, and went to every milliner and mercer, every seamstress and dressmaker at work in the city, and turned my lace into greenbacks.

. Fine stuff, they said, true Irish lace, handmade, not from a machine.

Lovely work this is, they said, beautifully made. Put your heart into it, didn't you?

Oh, they didn't know, they didn't know how I'd put my heart into it, they didn't know how I'd toiled on that lace, and what I'd tied it to, and what it had been meant to carry.

I went from one counter to another, watching them finger the lace with their long, hard fingers, watching them look at the lace with their hard-looking eyes, letting them take the measure against their arms and saying not a word as they hemmed and hawed and told me what they'd give for it. Some nine cents a yard. Some ten. One eleven. Most eight, for it was the war, dearie, money was tight and patriotic ladies were helping the war effort by wearing simple gowns, take it or leave it.

I never said a word to argue, only took what they

offered for as much lace as they would buy, and then left, and went to another, and listened to the same story again through the long July day.

And when I had sold every yard, I had seventy-two dollars and thirty-eight cents, United States currency. I stood me on the sidewalk outside St. Aloysius and looked at the money in my hands. Enough. It was enough. The setting sun turned the greenbacks to gold in my hand, and the stretcher men coming in and out of the church paused to look upon me and quiz me with their looks.

I raised my eyes to the church. I'd not stepped foot in it for a year, not since the first wounded man had been brought in. I stuffed the money into my pockets and went in.

The adornments of the church were a balm to my eyes, the paintings on the walls and in the chapels, the holy scenes and the saints' lives, and the flickering lights at the altar put a soft bright seal of starlight on the beds and cots of wounded soldiers that filled the aisles and chapels. Stepping light and strong as a boxer from one bed to the next was my Da, his hair white in the candleglow.

I watched as he bent to one soldier, and then rose and spoke with an aproned nurse, and she patted his arm and nodded twice, and pointed him toward another man in another cot.

"Mairhe, it's good to see you." Father Wiget came from the shadows of a chapel behind me.

"Our Michael is dead."

"God rest his soul. Did it take that much to bring you to your Da, Mairhe?"

"Yes." I bowed my head to him, and he blessed me, and my tears came at last.

So he took me to my Da, and without a question my Da put his arms about me and held me close, and I told him about our Michael, and how he'd died in the fighting at Gettysburg, and my Da said he'd always known it would be so. For he was a Mehan, wasn't he, and wasn't he raised to be a fighter?

"Like you, my girl. Like you."

"I'm not a fighter," said I.

"You are, though. You're a Mehan, an Irishwoman."

I caught my tears at that, and pulled forth the money from my pockets. "Ireland, Da. Here it is at last. I've brought passage home."

He touched the greenbacks with an unsteady hand. "God. God."

"You've dreamed of it long enough, Da. You can go home."

"God," he said again, and wiped a tear.

"I'll talk with Father Wiget. I know he can make arrangements for you. Are you well enough? You seem well now, Da. There's still cousins and all back in Sligo who can look out for you."

Da was shaking his head back and forth, holding both my monied hands in his. Then he looked up.

"Mairhe. You don't sound like a girl who's coming too."

"No. No."

From a cot nearby, a man laughed, and then coughed. The nurse at his side scolded him gently, and he laughed again, but softer. He was a broken man, but he would be put together and be whole again and he knew it and it sounded in his laugh. The man struggled to sit up on his cot, and held up his bandaged arm as though to say—see, already it's better, I'm going to be better. And the white bandage in the darkness was bright as a star, delicate as lace, strong as a dream. And so was the soldier.

And so was I.

# ABOUT THE AUTHOR

JENNIFER ARMSTRONG is the author of many highly praised books for young readers, including *Black-Eyed Susan* and *Steal Away*. She lives in Saratoga Springs, New York.